ULTIMATE SINS

A collection of twenty erotic stories

Edited by Miranda Forbes

Published by Accent Press Ltd – 2007
ISBN 1905170599 / 9781905170593

Printed and bound in the UK by
Creative Design and Print

Cover Design by
Red Dot Design

Also available from Xcite Books:

Sex & Seduction	1905170785	price £7.99
Sex & Satisfaction	1905170777	price £7.99
Sex & Submission	1905170793	price £7.99
5 Minute Fantasies 1	1905170610	price £7.99
5 Minute Fantasies 2	190517070X	price £7.99
5 Minute Fantasies 3	1905170718	price £7.99
Whip Me	1905170920	price £7.99
Spank Me	1905170939	price £7.99
Tie Me Up	1905170947	price £7.99
Ultimate Sins	1905170599	price £7.99
Ultimate Sex	1905170955	price £7.99
Ultimate Submission	1905170963	price £7.99

www.xcitebooks.com

Contents

Alice And The Red Queen
by Jean Roberta

Alice liked the roar of the power mower and the smell of freshly-cut grass. The trickle of sweat beneath her breasts and the pull in her bare arms and thighs made her feel like a real dyke, like the great tennis player who had hired her to groom her immense back lawn. Alice tried to ignore the throbbing of the motor as she wondered if she should consider a career as a landscape gardener.

Felicity Pakingham stood on her deck, gin-and-tonic in hand, watching the college student in shorts and halter top who rode her mower up and down the lawn, dividing it into neat sections. Felicity could see Alice's breasts bouncing from metres – or yards – away.

Squinting toward the sun, Alice was dazzled by the copper-coloured beacon of Felicity's very short hair. Ten years before, a sports reporter had named her "The Red Queen" after a merciless ruler in a fantasy chess game which had preceded all the currently-popular computer games by over a century. The name had inspired cartoon portraits of Felicity, including a computerized image of a tennis-playing queen. None of these caricatures did justice to the real woman's bold-featured beauty.

Felicity knew that she was slightly past her prime as an athlete, but her muscles were still sleek and hard. She could see that Alice was not used to sustained physical effort, but she could tolerate discomfort. The girl's pampered young curves and her determination both tickled Felicity, who smiled down as though at a worthy opponent. The prospect of an interesting game made her aware of her hands and her clit.

Alice looked up to see the enigmatic smile of her idol, and felt herself blushing.

"Would you like to take a break?" called Felicity in a voice full of hearty cheer, but with an insinuating undertone. "You must be thirsty. A cold drink will revive you." Alice almost fell off the mower in gratitude.

Climbing the wooden steps to the deck, Alice touched the cotton scrunchy that held her chestnut hair in a ponytail to keep it off her face. Even still, sweaty tendrils had to be pushed off her forehead. She wondered if her movements looked awkward to the Red Queen, whose body language was always elegantly direct.

"I have gin, scotch, beer and lemonade," offered Felicity, playing the hostess. "You may have whichever you like, but alcohol will make you feel hotter when you get back to work."

Alice couldn't look into the sparkling blue eyes of her idol. "Then I'd like lemonade, please," she answered demurely.

"You're a good girl, aren't you, dear?" purred Felicity, almost laughing openly. "Come into the kitchen. I'll get your lemonade from the fridge."

Standing in the cool, gleaming shade of Felicity's kitchen, Alice regarded the offered glass bottle as a welcome distraction. Felicity held the girl's outstretched hand in both of hers for a moment, and her touch felt electric to Alice. "You want to do a good job, don't you?" the Red Queen demanded.

"Yes." Alice gulped from the bottle as though her drink could make her articulate or competent, preferably both. "Of course."

Felicity ran a firm hand down Alice's drinking arm, making her shake. "What did you tell me you are studying?" she teased. "Not landscape gardening, is it? Pity this sort of thing isn't your forte."

Alice was devastated, even though she knew that the Red Queen wasn't completely serious. "Am I doing something wrong?" begged the girl, forcing herself to look at Felicity's face. Alice knew that her large, brown eyes must look hopelessly naïve, but she couldn't pretend that working for a celebrity didn't make her very nervous.

"Alice," Felicity addressed her as though speaking to a young child. "Come look." With a thrilling hand on the small of the girl's back, Felicity guided her onto the deck to survey her own work. "I appreciate that you're not finished yet," the Red Queen explained patiently. "But look at the borders of the lawn. The grass hasn't been evenly mowed, so you'll have to use something else to finish the edges. You weren't planning to do that, were you?"

Alice took in the lush expanse of grass and flowers. She didn't think the mowed area looked bad compared to her parents' lawn: the yard on which she had cut her mowing teeth, so to speak. But she knew she hadn't done a job worthy of a queen's castle grounds.

"My garden is my refuge," sighed Felicity, as if to herself. "I want it to be well-ordered, peaceful, soigné, private and discreet. Like a trusted companion." Her hand slid shockingly from Alice's back to squeeze one of her butt-cheeks and linger there, as if claiming the territory. Here it was: a lucky girl's wildest dream about to come true. Yet it wasn't happening in the way she had dreamed it.

"I'm sorry," Alice groaned. She shifted her stance, tingling under Felicity's hand. "Ma'am. I'll even up the edges. I'll do whatever you want." She took a deep breath, determined to speak her mind. "I know I'm not a professional gardener. I never told you I was. If that's what you really wanted, you wouldn't have hired me."

"Cheeky," remarked Felicity, who looked amused. She punctuated the remark with a light slap to Alice's behind.

The girl closed her eyes to break the Red Queen's spell, and awkwardly moved away from her. "No," retorted Alice, fighting off tears. "No. I'm not. Ms Pakingham, I admire you more than I can say, and I would be glad to take care of your garden all summer, for nothing. You have no right to blame me for not being an expert. You knew I wasn't a professional gardener or a tennis champion. I'm trying, but I wasn't born knowing everything that's important to you. I know other things. I've won scholarships in maths, which is my major. I can beat you at the video game that was named after you. And I'll still have a life after you've forgotten me."

Felicity was moved. Alice's anguish was heartfelt, even though she couldn't imagine how Felicity herself, whose victories had been cheered by millions, could fear being forgotten while she was still alive.

"Ah," breathed the Red Queen. "You don't want to be patronized." She smiled and pulled Alice into her arms, bringing her enormous relief. Alice felt as if she could come from being held this way.

The demanding warmth of Felicity's mouth on hers made Alice feel as if her bones were melting. Her grateful moan encouraged Felicity to part the girl's lips with her own gin-flavoured tongue and slide it into her mouth. Alice's lemonade had been abandoned for sweeter pleasures.

Felicity withdrew to let the girl catch her breath, but she pressed her crotch against Alice's belly and hip, letting her feel the hard object that Felicity wore under her Capri pants. The Red Queen held Alice's eyes with her own. "You *are* a lesbian, aren't you, my dear?" she drawled.

"Oh yes," grinned Alice. "I love – women."

"Would you ride a cock horse to Banbury Cross?" teased Felicity.

"There and back."

"Tell me something, Alice," cooed Felicity. "Answer honestly. If I'm not satisfied with your work, would you prefer to know that you'll never be invited here again, or would you accept a penalty to earn a second chance?"

Alice knew in her awakened clit, in her expectant bottom and in her swollen nipples what was coming. Nonetheless she asked, "What's the penalty?"

"A spanking," promised the Red Queen, slipping her fingers under Alice's shorts. "On your bare arse, over my knee. I won't patronize you by underestimating your endurance, my girl. Smart strokes can show you the error of your ways. No quarter asked, and none given. You won't want to sit down for a week after."

Alice knew that she should feel alarmed and insulted, but she couldn't help grinning or squirming. She wondered if she could actually come from the impact of Felicity's strong hand on her tender skin, or feel a returning gush of pleasure and pride while studying the damage with the help of two mirrors in the privacy of her bedroom. Peering into the dark rabbit-hole of her own perversity made Alice feel faint.

Felicity gave her girl's impatient young butt-cheeks a sharp pinch apiece. "You've made your choice, haven't you, dear?" she prompted.

"Yes," admitted Alice. "Ma'am." She didn't know what else to say.

"Then finish your work and do it well. Or you might not get a chance to redeem yourself."

The sun offered no mercy to Alice, but she was determined not to overlook a single, uncouth blade of grass. Suffering from heat of various kinds, the girl still had her pride. After she had ridden over the entire lawn, she took the mower to the tool shed and picked out a hand-held tool for trimming the edges. By the time Alice finished, the lawn was ready for a photo shoot.

She walked toward the deck, swaggering a little, as the other woman came toward her. "Beautiful," smiled Felicity. She was not only describing her garden.

"Anything for you," bragged the girl as the Red Queen held her glowing face in both hands and leaned forward to kiss her. Alice tasted her own salt on Felicity's mouth, and heard her own heartbeat.

Felicity withdrew. "Anything?" she challenged, looking predatory. "We'll see." She enfolded the girl in her arms and found the knot at the back of her neck that held her halter-top in place. She soon had it untied, and pulled the yellow top down to reveal plump, pink breasts. The girl's nipples were already hard and red.

"Here?" asked Alice, glancing at the high wooden fence which couldn't guarantee protection from exposure.

"Where else?" smirked Felicity. "My sexy grounds-keeper. This seems like the natural place for your ravishment." She rolled one of Alice's nipples between two fingers, squeezing it increasingly harder as the girl's breathing shook her ribcage. Before Alice could guess the next move, Felicity took the other nipple between her teeth and tormented it with her tongue.

The setting sun was streaking the sky lavender, pink and gold. Playful breezes stroked Alice's bare skin as Felicity unzipped her shorts and pulled them down. The dark hair between the girl's pale thighs was matted with juice. Felicity smiled as the unmistakable smell floated to her nose. Slipping two fingers into the wet heat, Felicity collected Alice's nectar for tasting. "Ohh," moaned the girl. "Make me yours."

"Really?" sneered the Red Queen. "Are you giving me an order? How presumptuous. What a greedy wench you are."

"Or leave me alone," parried Alice, standing proudly naked in the summer twilight like a nymph in an old painting. She had set her hair free, and it flowed over her tanned shoulders. "If I'm not good enough, tell me to leave. I'll never come back. You can pretend you never met me."

Felicity nodded curtly, in an almost military gesture of respect. She couldn't keep the smile off her face. "I'm greedy too. I want your mouth, my dear." The Red Queen efficiently shucked her clothes and her favourite strap-on cock, and left them scattered on the grass.

Alice knelt and paid homage to her idol's ginger-coloured bush with careful hands and a daring tongue. The girl was more confident and experienced than Felicity had expected, and she soon discovered how to make Felicity groan and buck. Alice's face was wet when she raised it again.

"You have talent, girl. You were meant to give pleasure. I want to know how much you can take. Like this, like the little animal you are." Felicity positioned her on all fours on the short, prickly lawn. "I have nothing to tie you with. Will you stay in place until I release you?" Alice did, and even spread her legs apart without being told.

The girl wiggled her bottom slightly while Felicity retrieved her valued tool and girded her loins. "This is what you want, isn't it?" she snickered, kneeling behind the girl and opening her wet cunt with one hand while holding her silicone cock with the other. She teased Alice with the head until the girl couldn't resist pushing back, wanting to be filled. With a well-placed lunge, Felicity sank in to the hilt.

"Oh, Ma'am!" Alice burst out in an agony of pleasure. "Oh!" She had more to say, but Felicity's catchy rhythm silenced her for several beats. The girl knew from experience that the ecstasy of surrender, the sweetness of feeling completely owned, wouldn't last. As she grew impossibly wet, drenched by the storm in her eager young centre, she wished she could record the experience and play it over and over whenever she needed to remember her brush with fame and power.

"It's – what we both want," the girl panted, squeezing

the object that seemed amazingly real. "You too. Say it. Please. Say it."

Holding Alice by the hips, pressing against her warm behind, Felicity felt blessed. She felt a transfusion of something like innocence or like hope from this girl who gave herself so willingly without giving herself up. Felicity fucked her roughly, knowing that anything less would feel insulting.

"I want you," growled the Red Queen. "Want you! Won't – let you – go." She felt a subtle change deep inside her girl.

The wild ride ended too soon for both. Alice's climax was like fireworks for an Amazon national holiday, while Felicity's was milder, being partly vicarious.

The two naked women sat entwined, watching the stars come out. "A video game might be named after you some day," mused the Red Queen, playing with Alice's breasts. "But you'll never rise too high for me to spank."

Alice felt a pang of despair, and wondered how she could ever have expected better treatment. "To keep me in my place? To remind me that I'm nobody in your world?" Her voice dripped with the sarcasm of disillusioned youth.

"Those intentions are hardly the same, sweet Alice," lectured Felicity, stroking her girl's tangled hair. Felicity sighed discreetly. "But certainly, you need to learn your place in my life. My meaning will sink in, I hope." And before long, it did.

Years later, a rumour surfaced in the tabloid press that Felicity Pakingham, having lost her edge, had plunged into a senseless affair with a young computer geek named Alice Liddell, a lesbian barfly with whom she had nothing in common. Felicity refused to dignify such gossip with a response, while Alice patiently explained to the nosy that she had formerly worked for Ms Pakingham, nothing more. And she always seemed completely credible.

Serial Satisfaction
by Cathryn Cooper

Michael ran his hands around the steering wheel as he drove. They were sweaty – with excitement. A throbbing expectancy ebbed and flowed in his lower torso.

Swiftly, he switched his lights from main beam to dipped. Ahead of him was the lay-by – their usual meeting place. Her car was already there. Just thinking about her dark hair, her sparkling blue eyes, made him breathe more heavily. Imagining her round and very full breasts and what was going to happen next, increased the aching throb between his legs.

Accompanied by a cloud of expensive perfume, Crystal, Thomas's wife, opened the car door and slid into the seat beside her husband's best friend. His hands left the steering wheel and grabbed her shoulders. He clasped her to him and they kissed long and deep.

'It's so good to see you, babe,' he said, his lips still pecking at her cheek, her ear, the soft waves of her hair. He smelt her freshness, her warmth permeating through his shirt to his skin.

The firmness of her body excited him. The smell of her invoked an odd feeling in him of wanting to ram himself into her as a knife slides into butter. He wanted to eat her, mould with her, savour her body in such a way that all his senses would be satisfied.

'I want you so much.' That was all that he said.

As her hands ran down over his chest to his waist and his zip, Michael threw back his head and groaned. She pulled his erection out the front of his trousers and began stroking it. Her head dropped to his lap.

Michael felt as though he'd died and gone to heaven. This was every guy's biggest fantasy; a beautiful broad giving him head. But she was going too fast. He was going to come too soon if she went at it this quick, and he didn't want that. He wanted to string out the time, make the most of it whilst he could. Too quick and it would all be over. He wouldn't be able to give her what she wanted and that was too sad for words.

'Crystal, can't you wait?'

A muffled 'no' drifted upwards. Through narrowed eyes, he could see the top of her head bobbing up and down in a steady tempo as her lips sucked on him. Her mane of dark hair hid his sex and what she was doing to it. Never mind. He didn't need to see. He could feel what she was doing, and it was absolutely delicious.

'That is so good.'

As he groaned with pleasure, he rested his hands on her head and adjusted his pelvis so she could get to him better.

Hot, moist kisses fell from her lips and all along his stem. Her tongue licked at his pubic hair and her hands pulled on him with a steady rhythm.

'Crystal… Oh Crystal!'

His voice had a drifting quality about it – like a breeze blowing rushes along the river bank. Like the rushes, he was helpless to do anything about it.

'Crystal. Slow down, babe. I'm coming too quick…'

The moment of no return was nigh, but just as he was about to ejaculate, she brought her head up.

'Have you told Josie yet?'

Telling her that he had done no such thing was not an option. She'd be mad. Might even bite it off rather than suck it.

By way of consolation, he tried to kiss her. She ducked away.

'Michael,' she said in an unmistakably forthright manner. 'I asked if you'd told your wife yet. We can't shag in lay-bys for the rest of our lives.'

'Oh come on, Crystal. We had guests tonight. Big-shot guys who I had to impress; Josie did a great job and anyway, before I could get her alone you rang and demanded I get out to see you.'

She turned her head as he tried to kiss her mouth again.

'You're full of shit, Michael. I don't know why I bother. I should dump you right here and now the way you treat me.'

Michael sighed and despondently rested his head on one hand. When Crystal had called earlier that evening he had immediately wanted sex with her. That was how quickly she could turn him on. He had come out with that specific intention in mind. Now, his penis was softening as the wetness her mouth had left turned chilly. What if he were to ask her to give him time, or mention the excitement of having sex in the great outdoors – even a lay-by. Would she change her mind and stop pressurising him to leave Josie and go off with her? He doubted it.

Crystal sat with her arms folded, staring out of the windscreen. Folding her arms made her look quite formidable. And her chin looked so square; like a prize fighter. Frightening!

Her red, glossy lips were fixed in a self-willed pout. Michael suddenly felt very vulnerable.

'Well. When are you going to tell her?' Her voice had taken on a certain cutting edge. Michael responded by squeezing his legs more closely together.

'It's not that easy, darling,' he wheedled and attempted to reach for her.

'Don't you darling me!'

11

She hit his hands away.

This was bad. Very bad.

Michael felt the cold getting to his exposed dick and his stiffness was going fast. He had an urge to put it away, but had a greater longing for her to go back down and give it the kiss of life. The likelihood of it happening did not look too promising – not for the moment at least.

But Michael wanted his own way and meant to have it. He softened his voice. 'Look, Crys. Tonight was full of business. The moment wasn't right, but it soon will be. Josie's off to Cornwall shortly. Instead of just screwing each other ragged during that time, why don't we go over things and get everything in proper order. What do you say?'

When she turned the full force of her eyes on him, he felt like melting – or coming in his trousers. His cock stirred, lifting its head slightly as though its one eye was seeking out whatever might be on offer.

Crystal was beautiful and knew it. Sometimes he felt as though he were falling into those eyes of hers. It was as though each sparkling glint was a chip of glass that burrowed into his flesh, pulling him closer to her like some weird magnetic field.

Slowly, the wilful glitter left her eyes. Her jaw loosened and the sculpted perfection of her cheekbones softened.

A smile returned. 'All right, Mike. When Josie's away, you and I will play. But we'll also make plans, plans for us; for me and for you. OK?'

'Oh, yes!' Michael placed his hands on either side of her head. He ruffled her long, silky hair as he gazed at her, and then sucked in his breath as her hands ran down to his open zip. 'Oh, yes,' he said again, his eyes half closing as his mouth met hers.

He was hot, he was hard again, and he was pretty sure that Crystal was about to resume what she had been doing so well.

With no care for his pride or his comfort, he felt his penis being pushed back into his pants. To his great surprise, this was followed by the sound of his zip being closed.

His lips left hers. 'What are you doing?'

She grinned and patted the bulge that pushed against his jeans.

'Keeping it for a rainy day.'

'But, Crys…'

She wagged her finger at him, tapped his nose, and then kissed it.

'Save it, buddy. Save it until Josie's away and we can get down to things a little more seriously and in far less restricted a space.'

'But, Crys…!'

Crystal was already outside the car. He got out too and ran after her before she had a chance to get into her soft topped, sporty Merc.

She rounded on him immediately, the same anger as before smouldering in her eyes. 'I told you before,' she said to him loftily. 'I want you full-time. So get to it. Stop messing me around.'

Michael stood with his mouth open, hands hanging useless at his side.

Panic suddenly grabbed hold of him. Crystal gave him true sexual satisfaction; he couldn't live without that, or without her. It was just about getting up the courage.

'I will see you when Josie's in Cornwall, won't I?'

Crystal tossed her hair so it fell over her bare shoulders and down her back like a black fountain. Her attitude was unyielding.

'Of course you will. I fully intend to have you Michael Warner – one way or another.'

He watched her go, her headlights searing through the darkness and making the tarmac of the road look wet as she drove swiftly out of sight.

There was a hollow feeling inside him, as though she had drained him dry. Crystal played with him. She lifted him up, and she let him down. She aroused him, and then left him stranded high and dry with a full-blown erection. It was still there now, hot and throbbing in his pants.

He walked back to his own car and drove home. When he got there, the house was in darkness. Josie had already gone to bed.

There was a blue darkness to their bedroom like the light they use in ghost movies. The curtains wafted gently before the open window.

Just as he'd guessed, Josie was in bed sound asleep. Her shoulders were bare and gleamed almost silver. The sheet barely covered her breasts. No matter that it was Josie and not Crystal, his penis responded to the sight of her. Crystal had left him high and dry. Now he wanted Josie.

Josie was sweet, like a flower, he thought – a neat carnation wrapped into itself with a silky stalk and slim-limbed leaves. She was fragrant and sweet but not as wildly heady as Crystal; not as dark, not as compellingly beautiful.

Yes, Josie was sweet, and tonight he was glad to have her.

He ran his hands down her back, felt the angular form of her shoulder blades, the nodules of her spine only barely covered by flesh.

As his hips pulsed against her and the tip of his penis nudged at her behind, his fingers followed the soft curve of her hip and the sweep of her thigh. Between kissing the nape of her neck and the indent between shoulder and ear, he murmured sweet nothings, told her how glad he was to have her.

'This feels good,' he said against her ear.

In his mind it wasn't his wife but Crystal he was doing this to. It was Crystal who had aroused him, Crystal who played with him like a cheap toy and then left him wanting. It was Crystal who had set him ablaze.

14

Josie did not waken. But Michael didn't need to have her awake. He was enjoying what he was doing; feeling her, using her without her knowing. It was a very singular thing. With closed eyes, he jerked his pelvis against her and when at last his moment came, he let his semen seep between the cheeks of her behind and run down to stain the sheets.

Just as she's staining our lives, thought Josie, still pretending to be asleep. Crystal, she'd decided, was like a stain ruining more than one life. This was not the first husband she'd seduced.

I'd like to wash her out of our lives, thought Josie, just as I have to wash this sheet in the morning. Michael too, she thought to herself. She wasn't into forgiveness. She'd set the wheels in motion, downloaded indecent images from the internet and onto his company files. Tonight before he'd gone out to see *her*, his business colleagues had been talking about a security scan taking place the following day. She smiled to herself. Well, they'd certainly come up trumps on this occasion.

As for Michael? He'd be destroyed, and would a disgraced Michael appeal to a woman like Crystal? She doubted it. Michael would have to rebuild his career and Crystal would move onto someone else.

'You're mine,' she whispered into the darkness.

Michael didn't hear, but carried on snoring beside her.

Shared Experience
by Lynn Lake

The first time David asked me, I said no. And the second and third time. By the fourth time, I got pissed off. "Okay, you want a threesome, I'll give you a threesome! I'll drag some perv off the street – a guy, mind you – and you and him can take turns fucking me senseless! How'd you like that!?"

He didn't. He sulked, and mumbled something about our love life getting stale and how I used to like to experiment and how wild we were before we moved in together; all valid points, I realised unhappily. Suffice it to say that he eventually got his wish. On the one condition that I got to choose the woman from the online catalogue at the escort agency that he just happened to have bookmarked.

So, I chose the woman; someone impersonal and professional, someone who would do her job, well, and disappear, not get involved beyond the physical. And, as I talked to the receptionist at the agency to set up a date and time, I wasn't at all surprised to find that my recently dormant feelings of burning sexual anticipation had been seriously rekindled: the trembling of the hands and voice, the cold sweat, the hardening of the nipples and the dampening of the pussy – the feeling that I was sexually alive and didn't give a fuck what the world thought!

Thus, by the time our sex toy for the evening arrived, I

was probably even more aroused than David. And he was plenty aroused; our preparatory hour-long, multi-positioned love-making session had left little doubt about that. I answered the doorbell before the first ring had dissipated. "Hi," I said to the young woman on the doorstep.

I felt my whole body start to shake slightly as I eyeballed the gorgeous filling to David's fantasy sandwich. She was green-eyed and blonde-haired, and her provocative lips were painted blood-red, her face delicate and inviting and pretty, her body curvaceous and outrageous. She had the unlikely combination of huge breasts and tiny waist – something you normally only see in porn videos and TV exercise shows. As she stared at me staring at her, my face flushed red and sweat pin-pricked my pale skin. I'd had a few lesbian encounters in the past, but nothing of her magnitude.

"Hi, I'm Cassandra," the super-sized supermodel said, shattering the awkward silence. "Can I come inside?"

Hopefully, I thought, hopefully. I smiled nervously, my mouth as dry as English wit. "Uh, sure … sorry, Cassandra. I'm Amy. I was the one who, um, phoned about you."

She nodded and slipped past me, and I caught the scent of her sweet, sweet body spray; caught it and held it and closed my eyes and revelled in it. It clouded my head, warmed my body, and left me vulnerable to any and all suggestions. This lady was clearly packing heat.

"So, where's the lucky guy?" she asked pleasantly.

"Huh? Guy?" I gave my head a shake. "Oh, yeah – the guy." I yelled, "David!" then escorted sexy Cassandra into the living room.

David burst onto the scene like he'd been shot out of a cannon, exchanged greetings with the main dish in our upcoming sensual meal, and then led her down the hallway and into our bedroom. After a couple of anxious minutes, he remembered that a threesome involved three, and ran back and grabbed my sweaty hand with a sweaty hand of his own. "You still want to go through with this?" he asked, feigning earnestness.

"Well, I–"

"She's one sweet babe, huh?" he interrupted, staring dreamily off down the hallway, his whole body twitching with excitement. I hadn't seen him so gung-ho since I'd buckled myself into a strap-on six months previous. "Not as good-looking as you, of course," he added hastily, licking his lips. "Man, you sure know how to pick 'em, baby!"

He dragged me down the hall to where Cassandra awaited us. Efficient professional that she was, she had already stripped down to her black bra and panties. "I thought I'd get comfortable," she said casually.

David and I jammed each other in the doorframe for a moment, then stumbled across the threshold. I coughed out the following words: "Uh, so … how should we get started? I mean …"

"Well, since this is David's party," Cassandra replied, gliding towards us, "how 'bout if I get started with … you." And she took me in her arms and kissed me on the lips.

I closed my eyes and let her soft, warm, knowing lips dissolve into mine. I hugged her buff body and opened my mouth and let her tongue roam inside. She explored my mouth and my lips, and then swirled her tongue up against mine in an erotic ballet that I wished would never end. We grew bolder and more heated and passionate, and mashed our mouths together, our breasts pressed tight against one another, my pointed nipples tingling with sensation.

The forgotten David inserted himself back into the picture by wrapping his arms around the both of us. Cassandra broke the seal on our sucking mouths, sending me headlong from heaven back down to earth. "I think we got David's attention," she quipped.

David was naked, and his hard cock was pressing into Cassandra's soft, tanned thigh. She guided him over to the bed like a mother guides a googly-eyed child into a candy store. She unfastened her bra and tossed it aside, and David fell upon her breasts and fed on them, gorging himself on her massive, bronze tits. She winked at me over his shoulder and said, "Come on, Amy, three's not a crowd."

I slipped off my shorts and T-shirt and was naked. I skipped over and playfully slapped David on the ass. He yelped and looked around at me, his tongue hanging out, Cassandra's tits glistening with his hot saliva.

"Here's how we're going to do this," Cassandra said matter-of-factly. "First time out, anyway." She quickly instructed her two over-eager sex students on the proper positioning.

When she was done, she was flat on her back on the bed. I was straddling her stomach and David was astride her face. He gripped the headboard with whitened knuckles, staring blindly at the wallpaper, his thick cock buried to the balls in Cassandra's mouth. I fondled her tits, rolled her swollen nipples between my fluttering fingers, and then bent down and sucked on her rubbery nubs.

Cassandra disgorged David's triple X erection and ordered me to pull down her panties. I pulled down her panties – and grinned.

It was only when David's ears finally cottoned on to the sound of me bouncing up and down on Cassandra, moaning more and more frantically, that he twisted his head around to find out what all my excitement was about. He stared, wide-eyed, at me, as I rode Cassandra's long, hard cock.

I smiled contentedly as his eyes flew back and forth between Cassandra's cock buried in my pussy, and his own cock buried in Cassandra's mouth. "Something for the both of us, sweetie," I groaned, already on the cusp of a mammoth orgasm.

His body signalled the agreement his mind was slow in acknowledging by convulsing wildly as his jerking cock sprayed white-hot semen into our transsexual's very talented, very versatile mouth. I quickly joined him in

Cassandra-inspired ecstasy.

Sweet Dreams
by Jade Taylor

Toyboys were just too tiring, thought Ellie as she stood at the bar, shouting over the noise to order another Red Bull. Sure, their energy in the bedroom was an undeniable plus, but the endless rounds of pubs and clubs first were tiring, never wanting to leave until all the lights were turned on and the bouncers were asking if you hadn't a home to go to.

They never wanted to just stay in, no matter what incentives you offered.

But Greg was such a cute boy toy, she thought, passing him his can. Six foot two with eyes of blue, toned and fit with a filthy laugh and a filthier mind, what more could a girl want?

She grabbed his head and kissed him hard, determined to make him leave early tonight. Though she'd been flagging moments before the kiss roused her, his hands running down her back and grabbing her butt to pull her tightly to him.

He was just so damn hot.

Greg pulled away to drain his can, then grabbed her hand, pulling her back to the dance floor.

Damn, she thought, so sure he'd been about to pull her out of the club, to take her home and ravish her once again.

She watched him as the throbbing beat pulsed through her body, swaying her hips to the music. Greg moved closer, holding her hips to pull her to him, then moving his hands up to caress the bare strip of skin between her skirt and strappy top.

As he moved against her she could feel his hardness grow; toyboys were so easy to turn on, so much more reliable for a hard-on.

Ellie snaked her arms around his neck, pulling him into a kiss, her tongue darting in his mouth, teasing him. He smiled as he pulled away, sensing her mood. His mouth moved to her neck, kissing slowly down to her bare shoulder, knowing the effect it had on her.

She lets a sigh escape, the fact that anyone could see their foreplay turning her on.

He looked in her eyes as he moved a leg between hers, pulling her closer as Ellie tried to pull away, aware of her skirt riding up around her thighs. He held her close as they continued, his leg between hers, rubbing against her, making her wet. His hands moved to her breasts, stroking across them, feeling them harden as they continued the pretence of dancing.

Ellie rubbed herself against his cock, certain that tonight she would make him leave the club early.

"Just a moment," she told him, pulling away and dashing to the toilets. Quickly she slipped off her sodden thong, stroking her clit once, then restraining herself as she straightened her skirt.

Surely this would do the trick?

She walked outside, disorientated for a moment as she saw that Greg had moved. Then she saw him, and sighed; he was with Adam.

Adam was cute; there was no denying that. But it was still tacky to have slept with friends, even if she hadn't known at the time. She didn't know if Greg knew about it, hardly a question she could slip easily into conversation.

"Hi Ellie, how are you?" Adam asked, kissing her cheek as she approached.

"Fine thanks," she replied, trying not to blush.

"I was just asking Greg if he wanted to come round mine, check out my new plasma screen and watch the game. You coming?"

"Sure," Ellie answered, though football and gadgets bored her she wasn't giving up on getting laid tonight.

The boys talked football in the taxi, and Ellie felt herself dozing off, only waking when they pulled up outside Adam's house.

"Make yourself comfortable," Adam shouted, going to fetch the beers as Ellie and Greg walked into the living room. Ellie lay on the sofa, placing her head in Gregg's lap. Now she wished she'd had more energy drinks, the vodka having made her feel flirty and drowsy. As she heard Adam moving around the kitchen she turned her head to kiss Greg's stomach, trailing her tongue along the waistband of his jeans, feeling him growing hard, until Greg stopped her.

Adam brought a tray of beers in and went to sit on the armchair but Ellie called him over, lifting her legs so he could sit on the sofa, her legs in his lap, her bum against his thigh.

She was so horny.

Her fantasy had always been to have a threesome, and though she knew she'd never dare in real life, the thought was guaranteed to get her off.

Greg and Adam would be ideal, she'd slept with them both before, knew they were open-minded and skilful lovers.

She imagined what they would do to her as she began to doze off, Adam and Greg glued to the TV and discussing football across her.

When she felt Greg's hand on her shoulder she first thought she was dreaming.

He stroked her softly, and she kept her eyes tightly closed as she felt it travel lower.

Sometimes in bed she would feign sleep as he began

25

touching her, refusing to open her eyes and 'wake' until she felt he deserved her attention.

Now she felt him touch her breast through her top, stroking around her nipples as they hardened in response.

Even with her eyes closed she knew Adam was watching, could feel his eyes upon her, unsure whether he was meant to see, whether Greg was taking advantage.

Like anyone could take advantage of her... Unless she wanted them to.

As Greg slowly eased the straps of her top down she felt Adam moving to get a better view.

Greg's hand travelled down to cup her breast, thumb teasing the delicate skin around her nipple. Already she could feel she was soaking wet, glad she'd removed her panties earlier. She shifted slightly as Greg began stroking her nipples, feeling her skirt moving up her thighs, hoping that Adam might see her glistening wetness and do something about it.

She felt his hand on her thigh and, still feigning sleep, opened her legs wider.

Ellie heard his sharp intake of breath, and knew he was looking, the thought making her almost abandon her pretence of sleep as she felt her wetness grow.

But no, she was asleep.

Adam's hands were less sure than Greg's, moving slowly towards their target; it had been a long time since they'd slept together and Ellie was Greg's girlfriend now, was this right?

Ellie felt Greg move and knew he must have nodded his encouragement, still the only noise she heard was the TV and their breathing growing heavier.

As Adam touched her cunt she had to bite down a sigh, her clit felt so sensitive already. She couldn't believe she was doing this, lying there with her breasts exposed, her skirt up and her cunt bare, letting them touch her.

Adam's fingers slid between wet lips, then deep inside

her, making her move her hips instinctively. Then he moved his fingers to her clit, circling it, teasing, making Ellie desperate for more.

She felt Greg move, and as she heard a zipper go she realised he had released his swollen cock. She could feel him stroking his cock with one hand as the other continued to tease her breasts.

Beneath her legs Adam moved, and a moment later she realised he too was stroking himself.

She felt so wet, lying there exposed with two men wanking over her. Her nipples felt so sensitive, and every time Adam touched her clit she was sure she would come, so close now.

Ellie wanted to tell them what to do, to tell them harder, faster, *more,* but was restrained up by the pretence of sleep, more effective than any bondage.

She felt Greg quicken his pace, knew he was watching her exposed body, watching his friend touch her, and that the sight was driving him wild, and he quickly came, spilling his seed across his lap and in her hair.

In contrast Adam's hand became slower, prolonging this, touching her so slowly, stroking his cock so slowly she felt sure she couldn't stand it any longer.

Then she felt his body shudder, spunk fall across her thighs, and she could hold it no longer. She couldn't help her body shaking as she came, gasping loudly now, Greg's hand pinching her nipples as Adam rubbed her clit harder.

Ellie waited a moment, then, as if waking, she yawned and stretched her still-exposed body across them.

"I've just had the strangest dream," she told them, standing and straightening her clothes. She held her hand out to Greg. "Come on, lazy bones, time to go home."

She leant over to kiss Adam's cheek. "Thanks for a great night. Sweet dreams."

Purposeful Liaison
by Shermaine Williams

Sitting on her towel, squinting at the sea, watching people having fun, she wondered whether she should have gone home with him.

It was supposed to be a break to enable them to reconnect, to have fun, to enjoy each other's company, but he had been called back to the hospital where he was a consultant. She knew it could be busy; she was a consultant herself, albeit in a different hospital, and it was all too easy to let work take over.

However, she had been able to put work aside as she felt it was important for them to spend time together; he obviously didn't feel the same way.

Of course, he had apologised profusely, promised to make it up to her, insisted that she stay and enjoy the last few days on the beautiful island, but he still went, without giving her a second thought.

They had only been married two years. She refused to accept that the romance had already gone; repositioning her sunglasses, she lay back and closed her eyes, determined to make their marriage work. It hadn't got that bad yet, it could be improved.

Operation Romance would begin in earnest when she got back, in the meantime, she intended to top up her tan and make herself look gorgeous so that Nicholas wouldn't be able to resist her.

Barbados was a beautiful island; the sun was shining, the hotel was great and, despite suddenly being alone, she was confident that she could still have a good time. If she'd have known he would be leaving early, she would have made an effort to initiate sex more; but she left it to him and they had only had a few nights of vanilla sex. Consequently, she was horny, but would just have to wait until she got home.

Feeling her nipples tingle at the thought of sex, she raised her head slightly and, sure enough, they were protruding, easily visible beneath the thin material of her bikini top; hurriedly turning over, she decided that laying on her front would save her from any embarrassment.

It took only a few minutes of laying there, the sun beating down on her back, before she decided that even a brief period of embarrassment was better than skin cancer and got up to quickly attempt to rub on some sunscreen, awkwardly bending her arm and still only reaching her lower back.

'Can I help you with that?'

Having not heard him approach, she started and whipped her head around, nearly causing herself an injury.

'No, thank you,' she replied to the indistinct figure, as she peered over the top of her glasses and got dazzled by the sun.

'Don't worry,' he continued, walking around to face her. 'I'm not some sort of pervert.'

Finally, she could see him properly; he was about her age, mid-thirties, with trendy, choppy styled brown hair and unusually green eyes; clearly proud of his wiry torso, he wore just a pair of long shorts.

'I'm sure you're not,' she conceded, giving him a tight-lipped smile and hoping he would go away.

'I just wanted to offer some assistance.'

'Thank you, I'm fine.'

Lapsing into silence as she resumed her task, she hoped he would take the hint and use it as his cue to leave.

'Where's your companion?' he asked, sitting down next to her on the hot sand.

'Excuse me?' her demeanour remained normal, though she was suspicious of him – can't he see the wedding ring?

'We're staying at the same hotel…I've seen you around.'

'My *husband* was called away.'

Instead of quickly scurrying away after making his excuses, he smiled wryly, holding her gaze until she felt uncomfortable enough to look away.

'Left you on your lonesome?'

'I'm a big girl, I can look after myself.'

In reply, he smiled, but said nothing for a few moments.

'I'm Matthew, by the way,' he smiled, holding out his hand.

Quickly calculating her options, she decided that she couldn't leave him hanging and maybe he was just being friendly; besides, he knew she was married.

She placed her hand in his, instantly feeling the soft warmth against her skin. 'I'm Charlotte.'

'Nice to meet you, Charlotte.'

'And you.'

They both fell silent as they watched people splashing about in the clear blue water, it took less than sixty seconds for it to become too much for her to bear; sitting in silence with this stranger was just weird.

'Are you here on holiday?'

'Yeah,' he turned to face her as he came back to his senses. 'Just thought I'd take a quick break.'

'By yourself?' she said, hopeful that his girlfriend would soon join them.

'Yeah.' Damn!

'So…' Here it comes. '…as we're both alone, why don't we have dinner together this evening?' Bingo!

'I don't think that's appropriate,' she replied, solemnly.

'It's not anything sinister,' he smiled slightly, his eyebrows raised. 'I just thought it might be nice to have some company.'

'Still, I think it's best that we don't.'

'Okay,' he gave a small shrug. 'I thought I'd ask.'

'Of course, thank you, it was a kind offer.'

Seemingly defeated, he stood up and brushed the sand from his hands. 'Are you sure you don't want any help with that lotion?'

'I'm sure.'

'Okay, Charlotte, maybe I'll see you around the hotel.'

'Yes, nice meeting you.'

Fixing her with his piercing eyes, he flashed a cheerful smile before walking away; she breathed a sigh of relief when she was sure he was out of earshot, and only turned to glance in the direction he'd gone after a few minutes had passed. He was slowly sauntering up the beach, the sinewy muscles of his back ripping. Shaking her head, she marvelled at his impertinence – no doubt, he thought he was God's gift.

Resolving to try to avoid him, she lay back down, enjoying the sun's rays caressing her body.

Looking at her watch, she was in two minds about what to do. Not that she minded eating by herself, but she had no doubt that Matthew wasn't the type to give up easily, and would probably insist on joining her if he was down there.

She stood considering her reflection; though she would never consider cheating, it was nice to think that she was desirable. Nicholas barely seemed to notice her; he was always busy at work or too tired from work.

Telling herself she was being ridiculous, she immediately left the room, before she had a chance to change her mind; there was no need for her to hide away, nothing was going to happen, she was just being silly.

Having slowed before entering the dining room, she had been able to scan it and saw no sign of him and, thankfully, she managed to finish her meal without having seen him at all.

Somewhat triumphantly, she returned to her room and walked over to the window to gaze out into the darkness, wondering what Nicholas was up to. However, a knock at the door a few minutes later quickly ended her musing. Though she had no idea who it could be, she didn't ask, and immediately opened the door, eager to satisfy her curiosity.

'Good evening, Charlotte.'

'Hello, Matthew,' she said tentatively, inwardly congratulating herself on being right about him.

'I wondered if you'd like to join me for a drink.'

'No, I don't think–'

'Please. I'm on my own, I'd just like a bit of company.'

His pleading gained him a doubtful look.

'We don't even have to go downstairs,' he said quickly. 'We can go to my room and raid the mini-bar.'

She looked at his face and wondered whether she was just being rude, maybe he was just lonely.

'It's okay, we can raid my mini-bar,' she relented, opening the door further.

'Thanks.' He stepped past her into the room, brushing his hand against her hip in the process. Though she felt the touch, on the basis that she believed it to be accidental, she didn't mention it.

'What would you like?' she walked over to the mini-bar after directing him to take a seat on the bed.

'Whisky, please.'

With her back to him as she poured the drinks; she could feel his eyes boring into her and tried to decide what to say to let him down gently if he tried anything. Though she really wasn't in the mood for a drink, she poured herself one anyway before turning to hand him his.

'Cheers.'

'Cheers.'

They clinked glasses and he downed it while she put hers down to turn the desk chair around to face him; by the time she sat down, he was putting the empty glass on the bedside table.

'So, how are you liking Barbados?' he smiled.

'Oh, it's wonderful, so beautiful and the people are so warm and friendly.'

'Yes, it's quite a romantic place.'

'Hmm,' she smiled timidly before looking down at her hands.

'I never would have left you here by yourself.'

Incredulous, she looked up to find his intense gaze fixed on her, as if he could see into her.

'Look, Matthew, I'm not sure what your intentions were, but I'm married...happily married.'

'Yeah, I've seen your husband. He doesn't strike me as a passionate man.'

Her mouth fell open as she stared in disbelief.

'And I think you're a woman that needs a lot of passion in her life.'

Outraged, she flew out of the seat, trying to ignore the fact that she could feel her face colouring. 'How dare you! You know nothing about me or my husband and have absolutely no right to say that to me!'

With that, she stomped across to the room and flung the door open, trying to make the hand that was holding the handle stop trembling. 'Get out!'

Unhurriedly, he got up from the bed and walked over to where she stood, stopping directly in front of her, forcing her to look up at him. 'See? There's some of that passion.'

Enraged by the taunt, she attempted to push him out of the door, but he caught her around the waist and swung her in front of him, making her lose her grip of the handle and pushed her back against the heavy door as it closed of its own accord. Her hand shot out, grasping for the handle, but he took hold of it and raised it above her head, holding it against the door.

He held her firmly and she couldn't release her wrist from his grip, she looked into his striking eyes as he silently considered her face.

'Get off me!' she ordered, through gritted teeth.

'After you tell me whether that wimp you call a husband can satisfy you.'

'What?'

He pressed his body against her and made her gasp as she felt his hard cock pressed against her belly.

'Tell me,' he whispered, bringing his face close to hers. 'Tell me that he can make love to you all night.' His lips hovered an inch away from hers. 'Tell me that he can make you climax over and over. Tell me that just looking at him turns you on. Tell me that he can get you dripping wet.'

She didn't know what to say; she was breathing hard, hearing his voice over the whooshing sound in her ears, her body got heated, her heart was pounding, he was so close, she could smell the whisky on his breath; her clitoris was throbbing.

She said nothing, he brushed his lips against hers and she submitted to his soft lips and ran her tongue over them before sliding it into his warm mouth, tasting the whisky and moaning into his mouth as his cock twitched against her, desperately seeking his tongue.

Still holding her wrist, he ran his free hand up her thigh, sliding her dress up in the process, and made her gasp with surprise as he roughly pulled aside the thin material covering her pussy; one of her arms was free, she could have pushed his hand away, but didn't.

Still holding her knickers aside, he left her disappointed as he pulled away from the kiss, wanting to watch her face. Only once he was looking into her eyes, did he plunge his finger into her wet pussy, making her cry out as her muscles tightened around him.

'Are you wet for me?'

She looked at him through hooded eyes, not knowing what to say, not knowing why he was teasing her.

'Are you thinking about me or your husband?' he whispered, brushing his lips against hers as he spoke.

Breathing hard, she pressed her lips against his, hungry for his mouth, but he pulled away as he began stroking her swollen clit, making her lean her head back against the door as she sighed with pleasure. She couldn't believe how good it felt, she didn't want him to stop.

He briefly crushed his lips against hers. 'Who are you thinking about?'

Again, she failed to answer, she knew that she should say her husband, but if she did that, he might stop.

Watching her face, he pumped his finger into her wet cleft as his thumb rubbed her clit, making her body buck as her moans increased.

'Tell me.'

'Oh, God …you… I'm thinking of you,' she panted.

Satisfied at having finally got the answer he wanted, he withdrew his finger, released her wrist and kneeled in front of her, swiftly pulled off her knickers and pushed her legs further apart as he hitched up her floaty summer dress, before running the tip of his tongue over her clit.

Liking the fact that the minor touch made her cry out, he set out to improve on it and grabbed her bum before plunging his tongue deep into her warm, juicy wetness, using his nose and his mouth to stimulate her. Digging his fingers into her soft warm skin, he lost his grip of the dress and it fell over his head, hiding him from her view as he continued to lick and suck her pussy.

Throwing her head back, a scream of ecstasy caught in her throat as her arms flailed about, needing something other than the smooth wood of the door to grip onto, her legs trembled, making her think she might collapse; hastily, she clawed at her dress, dragging it up to enable her to run her fingers through his soft thick hair, that wasn't at all stiff with styling products as she expected. Not that she could believe what was happening, but she had never felt to good; Nicholas so rarely went down on her, and even then, he didn't really seem to enjoy it.

Matthew held her tight, burying his face against her pussy, lapping up everything she had. She looked down at him, feeling the wave approaching, she held his hair tightly between her fingers as she thrust her hips forward, her clit being massaged as he ate her.

With a violent shudder, she screamed as she climaxed, gripping his head as he gripped her bum, drinking the resulting deluge.

As the echoes of the orgasm subsided, she tenderly ran her fingers through his hair as he continued to gently lick her swollen clit, standing up after a few minutes and pressing his twitching cock against her as he whispered into her ear.

'You taste so good.'

She didn't get a chance to respond before he picked her up, effortlessly carrying her to the bed and throwing her down on it, before straddling her and pulling her into a sitting position to pull her dress straight over her head.

Though his cock twitched hard, angry at being ignored, he appeared the image of calm and patience as he reached around her to unhook her bra before slowly slipping it off; he was sucking her erect nipple before the bra hit the floor, running his tongue around the bud before taking it into his warm mouth, pulling and pinching the other.

She looked down at the man sucking her nipples, the man she didn't even know, the man who was making her feel so good and instead of making him stop, ran her fingers through his hair as she submitted to the warmth of his mouth.

All of a sudden, he stopped and jumped off the bed, holding her gaze as he undressed.

As he came toward her, naked and standing to attention, her eyes widened slightly, the anticipation making her body tingle.

He held himself above her, parting her legs with his own.

'I love to feel your fingers in my hair.'

He didn't say anything more and eagerly thrust his engorged cock into her waiting pussy, making her scream, her hands flying up to hold onto his bum, digging his nails into him as he worked his hips in a figure of eight as he slowly pumped inside her.

He watched her as he slowly slid his cock in and out of her slippery pussy, loving how wet she was and the intense pleasure registered on her face. Between his desire for her and her being so tight, he wasn't sure that he could last long, but surprised himself, managing to gradually increase the speed of his thrusts until she was ready to climax. With her eyes closed, she continued to moan loudly as he felt her pussy tighten around his cock, and he withdrew until just the tip of cock was inside her. The lack of movement and no longer being filled made her open her eyes to return his gaze.

'Do you want me to stop?' he panted.

'Oh God, no!'

Though his merciless teasing took a lot of will power, he continued to hold his cock at her pussy lips until she could take no more.

'Matthew…please fuck me!'

Smiling, he plunged his cock back into her eager, hungry pussy, making her cry out as she arched her back, disbelieving how deep inside her he was.

The muscles in his arms were burning, but he barely noticed it as he fucked her hard, making his balls swing as he rammed his cock into her, determined to make her feel better than she ever had, determined to make her scream even louder.

She didn't disappoint; her orgasmic scream was loud enough for the whole floor to hear, he arched his back as he shot his hot fluid inside her, feeling her muscles tightening around his shrinking flesh.

Still panting, her mouth and lips dry, she didn't say anything as he flopped down next to her, neither did he; they lay together, sweaty and satisfied, neither minding the clammy feel of the other's skin.

Feeling comfortable, she found herself drifting off, and didn't know how long she was asleep before being woken by his tongue running up her spine, all the way from her lower back to between her shoulder blades. He then pressed his chest against her back, and wrapped his arm around her waist before whispering in her ear.

'Don't feel guilty, just think of it as a holiday fling.'

As she felt his weight shift off the bed, she turned to watch him put on his clothes before leaning over her to kiss her lips.

'Thanks for a fantastic night, Charlotte.'

Not knowing how to reply, she remained silent and just looked into his eyes, continuing to do so as he walked to the door.

'Bye, beautiful,' he smiled, before leaving the room.

He was gone. She couldn't believe what had just happened and, were it not for the gratifying throbbing between her thighs, she would have thought it was a dream. However, thinking about his words, she decided that he was right; it was a one-night stand, one night of fun, there was no reason for her to feel guilty, she wasn't going to see him again. It didn't mean anything.

She fell asleep, happy that she didn't have anything to worry about.

A week later, she had come back down to earth with a bump and wished she had taken some more time off so she hadn't had to go back to work so quickly. Instead of relaxing and getting over her jet lag, she was rushing to leave the hospital after a busy day, after having received a call from Nicholas. On the spur of the moment, he had invited a colleague back for dinner and asked her to pick up a couple of bottles of wine on the way home. Though she would have preferred it to be just the two of them, she vowed to play the dutiful wife and not let it show.

The living room door was closed when she got in and she passed it to join her husband in the kitchen, where he was busy preparing the meal.

'Hello,' he greeted her with a peck on the cheek before taking the wine. 'Let me introduce you.'

With his hand on her back, he lead her to the living room and as soon as he opened the door, she found herself stunned into speechlessness, her throat instantly drying up.

'Charlotte, this is Matthew.'

'Good evening, Charlotte, nice to finally meet you.'

'Oh, er, hello, Matthew,' she stuttered, automatically shaking his proffered hand.

'Right, I'll leave you to it while I finish cooking.' Nicholas left them alone.

Not quite believing that he was standing there, she stood silently staring at him.

With a mischievous glint in his eye, he smiled warmly. 'Nicholas talks about you so often, I couldn't wait to meet you.' He took a step toward her, his lips inches from hers. 'Although, you look very different from the photograph on his desk...maybe it's the tan.'

The Florist
by Eva Hore

The guy was fucking gorgeous. Ever since I first laid eyes on him I'd come in weekly to buy flowers from him. My house had never smelled lovelier. I wanted this man and decided that today I'd have him.

I knew he shut at 6.00pm, so I pulled up and parked a few shops down. When I saw him take in the sign I made my move. I entered the store breathless.

'Oh, John, thank goodness I caught you,' I said.

'Melissa, hi. Running late, are you?' he asked.

'Yeah. I need some red roses and I was wondering if you could help me word the card?'

'Yeah, sure. Who to?'

'Actually, there's this guy I fancy and I was thinking of sending them to him, you know, see what reaction I get,' I said, coming around his side of the counter.

He was resting on the counter, pen poised, waiting. I leaned in towards him; his aftershave mingling with the scent of the roses made my head spin. I'd worn a shirt, unbuttoned low into my cleavage, short miniskirt and high heels. I noticed he was checking out my cleavage.

I was nervous, my face flushed, my heart beat madly as my pussy began to throb. I pressed my knee into his. He didn't pull back.

'The guy works in a florist. Has the cutest arse,' I said,

running my hand over his.

'Oh,' he said, playing along. 'Does this guy know what a sexy thing you are?'

He traced the biro down my neck and into my bra. He pulled away the cup so he could see my nipples, giving one a few quick flicks with the tip of the pen.

'I'm not sure. I was hoping I could show him,' I said as seductively as I could, my tongue slipping out between my teeth.

'I think he'd be really interested in seeing what's under that skirt,' he said.

'Do you think he'd like this?' I said dropping my skirt to the floor and stepping out of it.

'I'm sure he would, especially if you bent over the counter, yeah, like that. With your arse begging to be touched, I'm sure he'd find you irresistible.'

I opened my legs as I braced myself against the counter. I was standing on my toes, my arse cheeks beckoning him. 'Do you think he'd move the g-string out of the way and go down and lick my pussy?'

'I'm sure he'd love too. Do you think you'd mind if he tore them off you?'

Before I had a chance to answer he ripped the flimsy material away. My pussy throbbed excitedly. I opened my legs wider, begging for his cock to enter my hungry pussy.

He ran his hand down my crack and over my juicy pussy. I ground my pussy onto his hand, allowing him to feel how wet I was. He moved in behind me, holding my hips firmly, pulling me back into him. I wiggled my arse seductively against his groin. I could feel his erection, so I pushed back harder.

I heard the zip come down and felt him fumbling behind me. I knew his cock was coming out. My pussy was getting wetter by the second and I gasped as I felt his knob probe me.

Now his fingers dug into my hips as he pushed his

massive cock straight into my pussy. I gasped at the size of it. Oh, God, it felt so good. Deeper and deeper he pushed, filling me up, as I pushed back into him.

His hands reached forward and tore the buttons right off my blouse, roughly pulling the sleeves down and discarding it on the floor. He quickly unhooked my bra and grabbed at my breasts, massaging them and tweaking my nipples.

Then he pushed me forwards towards the roses that were still lying on the counter as he humped me mercilessly. My hands shot out crushing the petals to my body. It was so wild. I wriggled and pulled away from him, turning naked in his embrace.

His head bent down to take my nipple in his mouth. He sucked at it cruelly, the pain turning into ecstasy as he released his hold and tantalized it with his tongue. Licking, long and hard, then flicking at it crazily, driving me wild.

'Do you think he'd like to fuck me on the counter, amongst the rose petals, where my legs could dangle off the edges or wrap themselves around his back?' I asked breathlessly.

'Oh, yeah, I think he'd like to fuck that hot pussy. He'd like to ram his huge cock in there and give it a pounding you'd never forget,' he said still buried at my breast.

'Then I think he should hurry before someone sees us,' I whispered.

'A bit late for that,' a voice boomed from the doorway.

It was his wife.

'Shit, Marcia, let me explain–' he begged.

'Explain, explain what?' she said, coming in and pulling down the blind over the door.

I still had my naked back to her. I turned slowly, my breasts heaving from the excitement of being caught. She was gorgeous. I knew he was married because of his wedding ring, but I didn't think his wife would be so good-looking.

She eyed me as she came closer. I tried to cover up my

breasts but it seemed pretty ridiculous considering the rest of me was naked. John, I noticed, was still standing behind me. He'd made no effort to put his cock away.

'So this is what you get up to while I'm home cooking dinner,' she said.

'Er, um…' was all he said.

I had a feeling I was in for something other than what I'd planned.

'Let me see her properly,' she said to John.

John pulled away from me as she came behind the counter. I turned to face her. She ran her finger down my cheek, over my breasts, down my abdomen and into the hair of my pussy.

'I see you're not a natural blonde,' she said.

Her fingers slipped inside my pussy. She removed them and smeared the juices on my thigh.

'So you fancy my husband, do you?' she asked.

I was speechless, unsure of what to say.

'I said, do you fancy my husband?' she said more firmly.

'Yes, I do,' I said smugly. How obvious was it, I mean I'd just let the guy fuck me.

'John, go and get some of that twine over there. I think we should tie her up while I think about what I should do about this situation,' she said, as her hand covered my mound.

She cupped my pussy while her other hand ran over my breasts, lingering on one nipple before giving it a quick squeeze.

'Tie her hands together, pull them over her head and lay her out on the workbench out the back. I'll be out there in a minute,' she commanded.

John pulled me by the arm into their workroom. 'Don't worry, she won't hurt you. She just wants to have a little fun. You're up to that, aren't you?'

'She likes it both ways, does she?' I asked.

'You wait and see. You won't be sorry she caught us,'

44

he said, tying up my hands and lying me on the table. He knotted the rope to a hook on the edge. I did wonder what it was there for and then he quickly pulled apart my legs, tying up each ankle and hooking the ends to the legs of the table.

He sprinkled rose petals over me and ran a thorny stem down my skin, scratching me lightly with it. Then he gently trailed the stem over my pussy lips and ever so lightly touched my clit. It sent electrifying shivers through me. I broke out in goose-bumps anticipating a night of raunchy sex.

'You like this?' he asked as his tongue licked my lips.

'Oh, yes,' I whispered.

'And this?' as his fingers explored my outer lips.

'Yes, yes, I do.'

'And when I tickle your clit like this,' he said, rubbing it, 'does it make you hot?'

'Oh, God, yes,' I could hardly breathe as he continued to rub.

'And when my fingers go in and …' he quickly pulled away as his wife's footsteps rang out on the wooden floor.

I lay there spread-eagled, my pussy dripping, wanting more, wanting John's gorgeous cock filling me up. My nipples were rigid, excited, as I lay there exposed in front of these two strangers.

She'd returned dressed in a leather outfit. Thigh high boots, short miniskirt and a tight-fitting bra. Attached to her wrist was a snappy little whip.

'Hmm, very nice,' she said, coming over to inspect me.

My body tingled all over. I'd never had sex with another woman before and was dying to see how it would feel.

She was running the handle of the whip over me, lifting my breasts as though judging their weight and then on to my pussy. She prodded at the opening, teasing me with the end of the whip. She opened up the lips with one hand and pushed the handle in with the other.

'You like that, don't you?' she asked.

I didn't answer, but my nipples betrayed me by becoming more rigid and I was breathing hard through my nose. She removed the handle and lowered her face down, only inches from me. My whole body throbbed in anticipation of her mouth, but she stood and turned her attention to her husband.

'You've been a bad boy,' she said. 'Take off your clothes at once.'

He did so immediately. His huge cock strutting before him. He had a magnificent body. All toned with great legs, that cute arse and of course his wonderful cock.

'Get down on that floor,' she commanded.

He didn't move so she flicked him hard with a snap of the whip.

'I said get down on that floor.'

This time he did and she strutted around him like a rooster checking out a hen. She lashed at him with the whip, welts breaking out over his back.

'When I tell you to do something, you do it at once, understand?' she yelled.

'Yes,' was all he said.

I was starting to panic now. Here I was tied up to the table, helpless with this madwoman calling all the shots. This wasn't how I expected to be introduced into my first bisexual experience.

'Get up,' she said, kicking at him. 'Get up and lick her pussy.'

He came straight over, lowered his face to my pussy and proceeded to lick me.

'You can do better than that,' she said, flicking his back.

He fell into my pussy, devouring it. It was the most fantastic licking I've ever had. His tongue was wild, licking up and down the folds, in and out of my pussy and when his fingers pulled the hood away from my clitoris I thought I would faint.

I was looking forward to his tongue doing the lambada on my clit, but he stood back, still keeping it visible and Marcia approached the table. She lowered her mouth towards me, her tongue flickering out like a snake, as she lightly played with my clit.

I was thrilled. Every nerve in my body seemed to be focused on my clit. The tip of her tongue teased me relentlessly. I tried to tilt my pelvis higher, I needed more pressure from her tongue but then she stopped all together.

'You like that, do you?' she asked.

She brought her red painted mouth to mine and now her tongue snaked its way in between my teeth. My scent was all over her and I latched onto her lips, my tongue exploring the inside of her mouth.

She pulled away from me. I didn't like to be teased. I wanted some action. My breasts were heaving as her mouth kissed my nipples. It was as though a feather was being fluttered along them. She pulled away and her warm breath was replaced with her teeth as she bit into the nipple to stretch it out.

I screamed in pain, and she laughed as she began to suck. Then John was on the other nipple attacking it in the same fashion as she did. It didn't take long before the pain turned into exquisite pleasure.

'Oh, yes, please don't stop,' I begged. 'Please don't stop.'

She began to pick the rose petals off my body with her teeth, dropping them in between my legs. On and on she went until she cleaned my body of them. Looking down I noticed stains from the petals where they'd touched my fevered skin.

She gave John a quick flick on his thigh. 'Up on that table. Assume the position over her mouth. I want to see how well this bitch can suck your cock.'

He jumped up straddling me and eagerly pushed his cock into my mouth. I gobbled at it hungrily, sucking, slurping, eager to please them both. He began to pump my mouth and I gagged as his cock grew to a new proportion.

Then I gagged and nearly choked as a hot mouth attacked my pussy. I was nearly delirious as I bucked into her mouth. I could hardly breathe, the combination of her mouth and his cock causing me to spasm into her mouth.

'Get over here,' she said, smacking John with her hand. 'Fuck this bitch and fuck her well.'

She stood back as John entered me. He fucked me like a wild man. His cock slapping in and out. His hands were underneath my bum tilting me forwards so he could get better access. My legs screamed from the pain of the twine but I didn't care.

I peaked again, screaming out with passion, my body saturated with sweat. I tried to get him to withdraw, I couldn't stand any more. On and on he fucked, driving me out of my mind. Finally he stopped, coming all over my stomach.

Marcia lapped it up like a cat at her cream. She came to me with his come smeared over her face.

'Lick it off,' she demanded.

I did. My tongue darting into her mouth to taste her. She began to moan and out of the corner of my eye, I saw John, on the floor between her legs licking her pussy.

'That's not bad, but let's see what your tongue can do for me,' she said, climbing up on the table and standing astride my head. I could see straight up her leather skirt and she was wearing no panties.

She lowered herself over my mouth and I was surprised to see such an unruly bush of pubic hair. It spread out towards her hips and covered the lips of her pussy. I had trouble getting my tongue to find its target. She practically suffocated me as I drove her wild.

John was at my pussy. He'd been licking and sucking and now I felt some probing and a hard object being inserted. I assumed it was the handle of the whip.

'Please,' I begged. 'Untie my legs and arms so I can make love to you more easily.'

'I call the shots here, not you. Shut up and keep licking.'

Her clit kept hitting my nose and I could feel it hardening. She raised herself until her clit was being rubbed on the bridge of my nose. She rode my nose like a woman possessed, coming in a rush, her juices dribbling down into my open mouth.

John had got his second wind and by the look of his cock I knew this wasn't over yet. He helped Marcia down and untied my arms and legs. Now it was his turn to lie on the workbench. I crawl up his body and took his cock deep into my mouth and from the side of my vision I saw Marcia approaching wearing a dildo.

I heard the scraping of a chair as she dragged it over to us. My arse was twitching in the air and a ripple of pleasure spread throughout my body as Marcia spread my cheeks. Her tongue was licking at my hole. Then she was at my pussy licking and slurping working her mouth up to my hole. God, it was fabulous. The dildo was knocking to come in. I'd never had it up the arse and tensed for a moment but it slipped in easily.

Grabbing John's cock, I pumped up and down the shaft wildly, engrossed with his knob as she began to fuck my arse. Pre-come was oozing from his slit and I licked it up lovingly, teasing him as my tongue snaked crazily over his engorged cock.

I could hardly hang onto him, my mind consumed with her fucking my arse. She pulled it out, flicking my cheeks with the whip, not hard, just enough of a sting to make it pleasurable.

'Up on his cock,' she demanded.

I stood up on the bench, only to lower myself down slowly over his cock. With my knees straddling him, she pushed me down towards his chest, giving herself a perfect view of my hole. Again she probed and as it was well lubed, she inched it in and began to fuck me in rhythm with John. With the two of them working on me, it took me no time to come again and again.

The three of us must have looked a picture up there on the workbench. Sucking, fucking and licking. It went on for hours before we finally stopped. With shaking legs I got dressed and left the premises promising to return the next Friday night.

It has now become our weekly night of fun. If ever you're going past the florists and the blinds are drawn but the lights are still on, and you hear some moaning and the occasional flick of a whip, you'll know what we're up to in there. And sometimes we even leave the side window open, so feel free to come and watch. Perhaps one day we'll allow you to join us.

A Lesson For Victoria
by Angela Meadows

My carriage jolted and lurched up the rough, alpine track making me uncomfortable as well as angry. I didn't want to leave home but I did understand my widowed father's reasons. Finding me in the arms of his stable boy was not what he expected of his 'little girl'. My lips still tingled with the memory of Bill's kiss and my nipples hardened at the thought of his hand pressed against them with just a thin layer of cotton in between. No, the real reason I was so upset was finding that the Venice School for Young Ladies, as father had called it, was miles from the city of canals – and up a mountain.

The sun was sinking behind the peaks at the end of a late summer's day as we drew up to a large, granite house with the distinctive steep roof of the Alps. The carriage door was opened immediately and my gaze fell upon a young man. He was wearing traditional Tyrolean leather shorts and his bare knees and strong thighs impressed me. It seemed that a swelling was forming in the tight leather at his crotch. I looked upwards past the loose cotton shirt, and found the blue eyes of the blond, smooth-faced young man looking at me intensely. He smiled, but it did not seem a smile of welcome, more one of anticipation. He helped me step down from the carriage. His firm grip on my wrist seemed to be a signal of possession as he guided me up the steps to a heavy, wooden door. He returned to the coach to retrieve my trunk. The door was opened by another handsome young man, similarly dressed but with black hair and brown eyes. He also gave me a thorough examination as he invited me to enter.

I stepped into a square hall carpeted with an old but thick Turkish carpet. A short, grey-haired lady emerged from a side room and advanced towards me.

"Ah, you have arrived at last." She spoke English with a French accent. "It is Victoria, is it not?"

I nodded.

"Named after your dear Queen, I imagine."

I nodded again.

"Come, take off your cloak and join the rest of the girls in the drawing room."

I felt the doorman remove my cloak from my shoulders. His hands brushed my neck gently and a spark of electricity travelled down my back. The little French lady was scurrying back to the room from which she had come so I hurried after her.

I entered a large, tall room with a window at one end. The setting sun was filling the room with light that reflected off the three huge mirrors that went from floor to ceiling on the other three sides of the room. Apart from cupboards in each corner, the room was quite bare of furniture. There was a large, wide couch in the centre of the room almost the size of a double bed and covered with furs. Some feet away from the couch was a line of six high-backed chairs. Five of the chairs were occupied by young ladies of a similar age to me. They all turned their heads to look at me but there was no sign of emotion on their faces. No doubt they were, like me, new to the school and wondering what was going to happen.

"Sit down, Victoria." The little French woman pointed to the empty chair. "The Principal is waiting."

I took my place and noted that the shape of the seat and

the hard straight back forced me to sit upright. I had barely adjusted my posture when a tall woman entered. She appeared to be in her mid-thirties. She wore a green silk dress buttoned up to the neck and had cascading locks of fair hair. The other girls leapt to their feet and I struggled to emulate them.

"Good evening, girls. Please sit." We sat down as one. "Welcome to the Venus School for Young Ladies." Did she really say Venus, I thought, or had she said Venice in a strange way? "I am Madam Thackeray, your headmistress. You have already met Madame Hulot, my assistant." She smiled and looked at each one of us girls in turn. "Here you will learn the knowledge and skills that will enable you to take your place in society as the wives of gentlemen. You will learn cuisine; you will study arts and music; you will discover the fashions of the day; you will practise the art of conversation and you will be taught how to run a household. These studies will occupy your days. In the evenings, tuition will turn to the art of attracting husband and how to satisfy him. Lessons will start shortly but first you will be shown to your rooms."

Madam Thackeray turned to Madame Hulot who opened the door. Six elegant young ladies entered the room. Each wore identical silk evening gowns in the fashionable new mauve dye. I gasped at the dresses as they left the girls' shoulders completely bare and revealed considerable décolletage. Their waists were extremely narrow and the skirts flared out. The six girls lined up in front of us.

"These are our senior girls," Madam continued. "They have a year of experience of our ways and will help you in your studies. They will now show you to your rooms." The girl facing me stepped forward, smiled broadly and held out her right hand.

"Hello, I'm your mentor. Come with me." She hooked her arm around my left elbow and guided me back into the hall and up a wide stairway. On the second floor we entered

53

a landing with doors on either side. My guide pushed on one door and we entered a comfortably-sized bedroom.

"Here we are, this is our room."

It seemed that we were to share a room and a bed, as there was just one ample double bed to be seen. I was surprised, but having shared a bed with a cousin I was not upset by the prospect. My mentor sat on the bed, scooping up the hoops and silk of her dress. "I'm Beatrice, who are you?"

"My name is Victoria," I replied.

"Named after the Queen, were you?"

I nodded resignedly.

"I expect you are hungry after your journey. You were rather late so missed dinner but a cold buffet has been prepared for you." She indicated a tray of bread, cold meats and cheese on a side-table. The bath is also ready for you, I'm sure you need one after your journey. I will return to help you dress in your school evening wear."

Having satisfied my hunger, I was enjoying a lazy, hot bath when the bathroom door opened and Beatrice reappeared. She looked somewhat flustered.

"Good heavens, Victoria, what are you still doing there? You should be getting ready or you will be late." I suddenly remembered that I wasn't on holiday but at a school. I was reluctant to get out of the bath and expose my naked body while Beatrice stood in the doorway glaring at me. "Come on, Victoria. Don't be prudish. I'll help you dry yourself."

She entered the room, picked up the bath towel and carried it towards the bath. I realised that she wasn't going to leave me alone so I made the decision to stand up and let her see me unclothed. The water cascaded off me. Beatrice examined me closely and I began to blush. Then she nodded with approval and I blushed some more.

"How old are you, Victoria?"

"Sixteen; seventeen in November."

"You look quite mature for your age. Your breasts are well-formed and firm and your hips are broad but your stomach is suitably flat. The men will take a fancy to you, I'm sure."

I wasn't sure that I liked this appraisal which made me seem like one of my father's horses but the mention of men made me think of Bill. He had paid my body compliments – the little that he saw of it.

Beatrice wrapped the towel around me and rubbed me vigorously so that I was soon dry. She tossed the towel to the floor and pulled me by the hand back into our bedroom. Clothes had been laid out on the bed, I presumed for me, but I was surprised at what they consisted of. There was a white satin corset – I'd never worn one before. Beatrice wrapped it around me and began to tighten the laces. I groaned and moaned at the unfamiliar constriction.

"Why do I have to wear this?" I gasped.

"Because it is part of the school uniform and because men like the figure it produces."

I was standing in front of a mirror and noticed that I certainly had more shape. My breasts were pushed together and upwards so that they rested on the top of the garment, my nipples on show. The narrowing of my waist also made my buttocks appear larger and more rounded than they usually did. Beatrice looked at my image and then at me. Her eyes descended and came to rest at my exposed mount of Venus. She passed the palm of her hand over my tuft of hair. There was a tingle inside that was unfamiliar. "You have quite a bush down there, haven't you."

"I have?"

"Yes, we need to trim that. Men don't like too much hair, you know." She tugged my underarm hair. "This will have to go too; it's very unsightly. Still, no time now."

She passed me a pair of white silk knickers which barely covered my bottom and, having made me sit on the bed, pulled white silk stockings up my legs and fastened the tops to clips at the bottom of the corset. She presented me with a pair of white satin slippers. As I put them on my feet she brought a long gossamer thin gown trimmed in white fur. I put my arms through the wide sleeves. The garment did nothing to cover me, but instead seemed to form a frame for my corseted figure.

"There; you are ready. No time for make-up, but that's all part of the course anyway. Come, it's time for your introductory lesson." Beatrice tugged on my hand, and dragged me out on to the landing. We almost ran to the stairs, my gown flaring out behind me. I felt as if I had no clothes on at all and wondered what sort of school I had come to.

We reached the room where we had first met. Beatrice pushed me in and departed. Like before, my classmates were already sitting there but this time they and I were identically dressed. I took my place in the uncomfortable chair at the end of the row and looked around me. The curtains had been drawn as night had now fallen. Many oil lamps had been lit so that the room was very light. A large candelabra dangled over the fur-strewn couch.

"Ah, you have joined us at last, Victoria," said Madame Hulot impatiently. "Punctuality is a virtue we foster here. Gentlemen do not like to be kept waiting." She left and a few moments later Madam Thackeray swept in, beaming at each of us new girls.

"Wonderful, girls. You now look as though you belong here and are ready for your instruction to begin. This evening you have nothing to do but watch. I want you to concentrate on what you will see and what I have to tell you. You will observe certain techniques which you will be studying during your time here so do not worry if you do not understand tonight."

I had no idea what she was talking about but as she moved to take a seat at the side of the room Beatrice reappeared and without looking at Madam Thackeray, or the six of us, she went to stand by the couch and looked at herself in the large glass mirror that was behind it. A moment later a young man entered the room. I recognised him as the blond servant who had helped me from the carriage. Now, however, he was wearing evening dress and looked exceptionally smart and aristocratic. I wondered about the meaning of his change of attire but things soon started to happen. He stepped up behind Beatrice, put a hand on her bare shoulder and spun her around. When she faced him he bent his neck and placed his lips on hers.

"For the purpose of this evening's demonstration, ladies, you must imagine that Eric is the man that Beatrice wishes to marry and that he desires her as his wife." Madam's words seemed to provide some explanation for the deep kissing that was going on. I presumed that we were watching a theatrical performance with Eric and Beatrice as the actors. However, the manner in which they clung to each other and inserted tongues into each other's mouths did seem to go beyond the realms of acting that I was familiar with. Bill had only placed his lips on mine, but as I watched I began to wish that we too had pressed our mouths as close together.

The pair parted and Eric began to undo the buttons on Beatrice's gown which conveniently for him, were situated at the front.

"Men often find the small buttons of a gown difficult to undo, so you must learn to assist discreetly," Madam continued. Indeed Beatrice had assisted so quickly that the gown had slipped to the floor and she revealed not the white corset that I and the other girls wore, but a blood red garment with black lacing. Beatrice now turned her attention to Eric.

"You will also have to acquire the skill of undoing the fastenings of the male vestments."

Beatrice certainly had the skill because Eric was swiftly divested of his jacket, stiff collar, shirt and trousers. In the same time he had kicked off his shoes and stockings. He wore no underclothes.

For the first time in my life a man stood naked in front of me, but his attention was on Beatrice. His buttocks were white, firm globes and he stood with his feet a little apart. He gave Beatrice a gentle push and she fell back on to the couch. Now I could see in the mirror beyond them, the front of Eric's body. He had a strong muscular chest but my eyes were drawn to his member which was as firm as a broom pole and stood out at right angles from his body. I never knew that it could become so large. The tip was a shiny purple and shaped like a massive toadstool.

"As you can see, it takes little to arouse a man. The skill comes in prolonging the arousal and giving satisfaction."

Beatrice had by sleight of hand unfastened her stockings, so now when Eric took hold of the vivid red knickers, he was able to pull them off in one swift, fluid movement. Beatrice spread her legs wide and bent her knees, pulling her feet up onto the couch.

From my position at the end of the row I had a full few of her sex, despite Eric standing just a pace from her. I saw that she indeed had far less pubic hair than myself and that it was trimmed into a neat arrowhead pointing at the cleft between her legs. Without thinking, my hand moved between my legs and like Beatrice's I could feel my outer lips swelling and a dampness penetrating my knickers. Her swollen crack glistened with her excitement. Eric knelt between her legs and lowered his head towards her sex. I saw his tongue stick out and lap at the juices oozing from her fanny.

"Not all men have a liking for cunnilingus, but many do. By offering herself, Beatrice has given Eric the encouragement he needs and for as long as he remains drinking at the trough so to speak, he will retain his erection and derive great pleasure. It is important that the lady also derives satisfaction from the process as she must retain her own level of arousal and lubrication."

Beatrice evidently was enjoying the experience because she moaned at each flick of Eric's tongue and thrust herself at his mouth. He gripped her buttocks, held her firmly and pushed his face hard into her groin. I almost felt as if I was Beatrice and his tongue was exploring deeper and deeper up my love canal.

Eric withdrew, drawing breath, and stood to stretch his back. Beatrice immediately slid from the couch to kneel in front of him. They slickly turned side on to their audience. Now I and my fellows could see Eric's long, stiff cock (the word I recalled Bill had used for his sex). It stretched to within an inch of Beatrice's face. She poked out her tongue and gently touched the tip. It trembled and Eric mumbled something, a 'Ja', I think. Beatrice leaned forward, carefully opening her mouth to surround the red onion at the end of the penis. I gasped as I saw it slowly disappearing into Beatrice's mouth. She kept her jaws wide apart as she took more and more of it into her mouth. She stopped with her small pert nose almost buried in his pubic hair.

"Beatrice is one my most skilled pupils in fellatio. Very few ladies can take the full length of a man's erect penis but some like Beatrice are able to open their throat and avoid gagging. The heat and the softness of the woman's mouth bring intense pleasure to the man."

Eric was indeed moaning and there was a tremor in his knees. Beatrice rocked back slowly and the shining wet penis re-emerged, but that was not the end. Now she started moving her head to and fro, in turn enveloping and revealing the member. As the glowing tip emerged from her lips her tongue played around it before it disappeared again into the depths of her gullet. Steadily, she increased the frequency of her movements. Eric sighed and groaned and began to shake. His testes in their sac wobbled and swung from side to side. Beatrice reached up and grasped them in her hand holding them firmly as her head now oscillated up and down the shaft. My hand was now pressed hard against my sex, rubbing in time with Beatrice's movement. I was hot and perspiring so much that I felt rivulets of water running down the cleft between both my breasts and my buttocks.

"Stamina is needed for this stage in the act. Some men reach satisfaction very quickly but many are lucky enough to be able to withstand the agony of pleasure for some time." Beatrice showed no sign of tiring. Her lips were now locked firmly round Eric's cock as it slid in and out. At last, when even I was beginning to feel exhausted, Eric let out a cry. I saw Beatrice gulp and swallow and immediately stop her movements. She remained kneeling holding the penis in her mouth, sucking gently.

"Some men like to withdraw at the point of orgasm and expend their semen in the woman's face. A number of women prefer that to swallowing the fluid, but in the spur of the moment you rarely have much choice in the matter. A warning though. After orgasm, the male often finds their penis rather tender. Be careful not to let your teeth cause pain." Beatrice reluctantly let Eric pull his penis from her mouth. It flopped, shrunken and wet between his legs.

"Young men take a few minutes to recover before they can embark on further lovemaking so this provides us with a break in the proceedings. I was pleased, girls, to see that you were watching intently. I noticed also that one or two of you were driven to pleasure yourselves by the excitement of what you saw. I hope you are able to remain dispassionate and observe the skills that Beatrice displayed. Over the next two years you too will learn these techniques. That is our objective here at the Venus School for Young Ladies."

Now that I realised that my new school was named after the goddess of love and not a watery city I wondered how my darling father could have got so confused. Did he have any idea of the curriculum I was to study? Reflecting on the emotions I felt as I had watched Beatrice give and receive pleasure, I was excited by the prospects that lay ahead. I thought of what I could offer Bill or any other eligible young man once I had completed my education.

"Now as Beatrice has had a chance to draw breath we will continue with proceedings. As Eric had been temporarily incapacitated we will have a substitute."

Beatrice had relaxed onto the couch and Eric gathered up his clothes and left. As he departed the other young man that I had met entered. He made his entry naked with his cock already pointing the way forward. He moved towards the couch. I sat up straighter and peered avidly at the pair. My fingers slipped inside my knickers and felt the slick wetness between my pussy lips. I looked forward with gleeful anticipation to what scenes of lovemaking would unfold before my eyes.

Story Telling
by Jim Baker

Part One

The Lecturer.

Cheryl walked along the corridor, her flat shoes making a gentle slapping sound on the tiled floor. She had gone all the way out to her car before she realised the keys were still in the laboratory, and she'd trudged back to fetch them.

The university labs were empty. The only person she'd seen was old Judd, the crotchety caretaker, on the stairs. As usual he had responded to her "Goodnight, Mr Judd" with a monosyllabic grunt.

Although Cheryl had worked in the department for two years it was clear old Judd thought she was too young to be a lecturer, and her being the only American teaching in an English university science department obviously made it worse.

'Bet the old bastard turned round and watched my butt going downstairs, though,' she thought to herself, grinning. She was several years younger than any of the other female lecturers and she had caught Judd eying her legs more than once.

Not that she needed old Judd's attention. Her blonde hair, slim figure and easy-going ways made her very popular and as an American, she was an exotic conquest for the locals. Her love life had been more than full during her time in England.

She sighed and walked on, thinking about Tony, the post-doc with whom she'd recently finished a three-month affair. He'd been offered a position in London, far too good to turn down. She missed him badly.

"Or, if I'm honest, I'm missing the feel of his cock in my pussy and his tongue in my mouth," she muttered, and then laughed out loud. "Or the other way around."

She carried on walking and grinned as she recalled her first time with Tony. It was mid-afternoon and they'd just had a coffee together. Cheryl had fancied him for a while and had been deliberately provocative with both her conversation and body language in the coffee shop. They were walking through the old tower of the university amid streams of students hurrying to lectures, when Tony grabbed her hand and pulled her into a corridor leading off the main building.

He led her about twenty yards along the curving passage then stopped as they reached a shallow alcove in the wall. They were invisible from the main area, but the chatter of the students still reached them clearly. Tony pushed her into the opening with her back up against the stone wall and neither of them spoke as they fell into an embrace, their lips locked together. Cheryl ground her lower body against his and sucked his tongue into her mouth.

They stayed, pressed hard together, and then Cheryl felt him move back. His hand slid under her short skirt and she moaned deep in her throat as he rubbed the front of her panties. She was already soaking wet and she moved her legs apart as his fingers worked the silk aside. Frantically she groped at the front of his trousers and tore the zip down. She found his cock and tugged it free, pulled it towards her, and lifted herself on tip-toe as she guided it past the silk and up inside her.

They broke the kiss and their eyes locked together as he thrust furiously, ramming her back against the hard, stone

64

wall. It was over very quickly. Cheryl felt waves of pleasure rippling through her at the same moment Tony gasped as he came. They were both panting as if they'd sprinted a hundred meters. Cheryl recovered first and gave him a quick kiss on the lips.

"We'd better put that away," she murmured, tucking his cock back in his trousers and zipping them up.

They walked hand in hand back to the main building without speaking. Just before they separated to go to their separate lecture theatres, they kissed again.

"Five o'clock in the car park," Tony whispered in her ear.

Cheryl found it difficult to keep her mind on her work as she lectured to her class of undergraduates, wondering what they would think if they knew their teacher was still sopping wet from a quickie in the corridor.

Her reverie was broken by the sound of voices and suppressed giggling from a corridor on her right. Cheryl stopped and took a couple of paces back, just in time to see the door of a lecture hall closing at the far end.

She slipped her shoes off and, carrying them in her hand, walked down the corridor to where she could see into the room through a window.

Inside were Steve Rogers, one of her third-year students, and two girls she didn't know, a blonde and a red-head.

Cheryl's first instinct was to march in and demand to know what they were up to but as she hesitated it quickly became very obvious.

Steve put an arm around each girl's waist, pulling them tightly up against him. Cheryl watched as he began kissing the blonde, while the red-head massaged the front of his jeans. The kiss lasted a long time and then without releasing his grip on either girl he turned his attention to the red-head and locked his lips on hers. As they kissed he moved back very slowly, the girls moving with him, until his buttocks were pressed hard against the back row of wooden seats and his legs were splayed apart.

The blonde undid the buttons of his shirt, slipped her hand inside and stroked his chest. Cheryl stood entranced, hardly daring to breath, although she was pretty sure they wouldn't have noticed had she burst into song.

The kiss finally ended. The boy let go of the red-head's waist and whispered in her ear. Cheryl heard her giggle as she slid down on her knees between his legs, her fingers already busy on his belt.

He began kissing the blonde again while the fingers of his free hand undid the buttons of her blouse and pulled it from the waist-band of her skirt. He eased his hand behind her to unhook her bra and fondled a breast as it dropped into his hand. By now his belt was hanging loose and the top of his jeans was open. The kneeling girl pulled the zip down, wriggled her fingers inside and a long, stiff cock sprang into view.

Cheryl licked her dry lips. The sight of the hard rod of flesh reminded her again of that first day with Tony. They had driven out of the car park with her fingers already working on his zip, and his cock had leapt into her hand before they had travelled a hundred yards.

Tony turned off the road into the local park and they ran, hand in hand like two kids, to the closest clump of bushes. He pulled her down on to the grass, his cock still sticking out of his trousers. She grabbed it as he tugged her panties down and tossed them aside. Her legs opened wide as he moved on top of her and slid inside with one long, hard thrust.

Cheryl reached her hand down under her skirt as the red-head pulled the jeans and underwear down to the boy's knees, took his cock between her fingers and kissed the tip. She slid her hand up and down the shaft, then cupped it around the balls that hung below and lowered her head.

She ran her tongue around the bulbous head, took it in her mouth and her head began bobbing rhythmically up and down.

Cheryl worked her fingers under the waistband of her panties and down through her damp pubic hair. She looked back at Steve. His lips had replaced his fingers on the blonde's breast and his hand was under her mini-skirt, stroking the front of a pair of white panties. She watched him fondling the tightly stretched silk between the girl's thighs, gently at first then more firmly until her legs parted. He pushed the panties aside and thrust first one, then two fingers inside her. His other hand was on the back of the other girl's head, stroking her red hair.

Cheryl fingertips found her clitoris and she stroked herself feverishly as she watched his fingers moving in and out, slowly at first and then faster until suddenly there was a muffled scream and the blonde's body arched violently backward. Seconds later there was a yelp from the boy and his knees sagged as he came in the redhead's mouth.

It was enough to send Cheryl over the top and she groaned and doubled up as the orgasm hit her. She stood gasping for breath for a moment then, gathering her wits, ducked into the room opposite and stood out of sight, holding the door just ajar.

After a few minutes the two girls came out together, looked up and down the corridor and hurried away, whispering.

It was a few minutes more before the boy emerged.

She let him get a few yards away before she stepped into the corridor behind him and mustered the sternest voice she could.

"Steven!"

He stopped dead and spun around, white-faced.

"Doctor Bridges!"

"What are you doing here at this time, Steve?"

He stuttered something about leaving his notes in the

lecture hall.

Cheryl raised her eyebrows.

"And the girls were helping you search, were they?"

He looked devastated.

"You were watching?"

"Yes, Steve. I've been here all the time. Lecture halls aren't designed for orgies, you know."

He looked down at the floor, face scarlet with embarrassment.

"So what do you think I should do, Steve?"

He shuffled his feet.

"I don't know. I don't want the girls to get into any trouble."

Cheryl laughed out loud.

"I don't think what you did in there will get them into trouble. Not in the old fashioned sense, anyway."

There was silence for a moment then he looked up at her again, concerned.

"What are you going to do?"

She picked up her shoes and gestured at the open door.

"Go back in there."

Cheryl closed the door and bolted it. Steve stood, looking warily at her like a wild animal ready to run.

"You won't tell anyone, Dr. Bridges?" he said hopefully.

"That depends on how good you are, Steve."

"How good I am?"

"Yes, Steven," Cheryl said softly.

She unzipped her skirt, let it fall to the floor and walked towards him.

"I'm sure you can be very good indeed if you try…"

Part 2

The Librarian.

… *"very good indeed if you try…"*

As he finished the last sentence Alan dropped his pen on

68

the table and leaned back in the hard wooden chair. He locked his hands behind his head, stretched hard and heard his joints crack. As he closed his eyes he felt hands massaging his shoulders and he sighed with pleasure.

"We're closing, mister author. I gotta throw you out."

Alan opened his eyes and focussed on the clock as the fingers continued to knead his muscles. The massage stopped and the girl sat down in the chair beside him.

"We're the only ones left," she said. "The librarian and the writer. I gotta clear up and lock up."

He shuffled the papers into a folder and put his pen in his shirt pocket.

"Sorry, Susie," he said. "Time flies when I'm writing."

"That's okay." She stood up. "What are you writing about?"

"Oh, just a story about an girl from the States who gets a job as a lecturer in an English university."

"May I read it?"

Alan had been using the library as a place to write his stories since the end of the summer. It was a lot cheaper than heating and lighting his small apartment. Susie was usually on duty in the evenings and they had become friendly, occasionally having a drink together in a bar near the library.

She was a private sort of person and Alan knew little about her other than she lived alone following a disastrous marriage. She had never seemed interested in his writing before so the request came as a surprise.

He hesitated.

"Well, it's a bit, er, racy."

Susie laughed loudly.

"And I'm a virgin? Come on, let's have a look."

She walked around, reading as she went, putting books back on shelves and straightening magazines in the racks. Gradually she slowed until she was standing still, just reading, then looked across at him and grinned.

"Well, well," she murmured, "ain't you a surprise?"

She handed back the folder and looked quizzically at Alan.

"Fancy a drink tonight, mister author?" she asked and without waiting for a reply took him by the hand and led him outside, switching off the lights and locking the door behind her.

"Where are we going?" Alan asked as Susie pulled him across the car park in the opposite direction to the bar, stopping when they arrived at an old, dilapidated Chevy.

"Tell me, Alan," she said as she unlocked the car. "Are you any good at undoing buttons and unhooking bras, or do you just write about it?"

He gaped at her

"Front seat or back, honey?" she whispered seductively and laughed out loud at the bewildered look on his face.

"Come on, Alan, get in the front. We're going over to my place for a drink. You can find out if all those things you've written about really happen or not!"

Twenty minutes later he was sitting in her apartment, a glass of wine in his hand, listening to jazz on the stereo. Susie had vanished into the bedroom after pouring drinks. She had insisted on taking the folder with her.

When she emerged she was wearing a long silk robe. She'd let her dark hair down around her shoulders and looked very different to the librarian he was used to. She poured them a second glass of wine and dropped the folder in his lap.

"You know," she murmured, "I imagined you were writing boring stuff about fishing, or how to play bridge, or house painting. And all this time it was this sexy stuff."

She sat down beside him and he smelled her perfume as she clinked her glass against his.

"And guess what, honey?" she whispered. "It really turns me on."

She moved closer, took the wine glasses away and put

her lips against his ear.

"I've made it easy for you," she murmured. "No buttons, no hooks. Just a belt to undo."

Her tongue tickled his ear and he shivered.

His hands seemed to move themselves and as the robe fell away he cupped her full breasts, fondling and sucking her nipples until she groaned with pleasure and fell back into the cushions, pulling him down with her.

"Have you got a long, hard cock like the kid in your story, Alan?" she whispered as she took his hand down between her legs and guided his fingers inside her panties.

He began to explore the hot wetness between her thighs and he felt her cool fingers freeing his cock from the confines of his pants. Their mouths came together, tongues duelling and her body writhed as his fingertips flickered over her swollen clitoris. Her hand squeezed his cock and began to move up and down, faster and faster…

Part Three

The Author.

… *"faster and faster…"*

I stopped reading, removed my spectacles and dropped the manuscript, no longer able to ignore what was happening.

"Godammit, woman," I growled in mock anger. "You're supposed to be listening to the stories and offering critique, not playing with my cock."

Joanne chuckled, her hand working skilfully beneath the sheet.

"Listen, mister author." she said. "This stuff is supposed to turn people on, yeah?"

"Yep."

"Well believe me it does. I've been playing with myself since the red-headed girl got young Steve's dick out. Feel."

She took my hand and guided it down. She was soaking wet and she groaned as my fingers touched her.

"So what do you think of the stories?"

71

"Fuck the stories! I want the real thing, not the stories."

I began to stroke her very slowly.

"But I do hope you let Alan fuck the librarian."

I took my hand away and picked up the manuscript again, pretending to study it closely.

She gave a yelp of frustration.

"Don't stop!"

"But baby, you've just made such a good point. Do you think Alan should fuck the librarian?"

"Yes! No! I don't care! I want you to fuck me!"

I dropped the papers on the floor and ran my fingers over her stomach and down between her legs. She wriggled and groaned as my fingers teased the soft flesh.

"I think Alan should suck the librarian's nipples."

She made little mewing sounds in her throat as I lowered my lips to her breasts, while my fingertips flickered over her clitoris.

After a couple of minutes I raised my head again, fingers still working.

"Do you think Alan can make her come if he just plays with her clit?"

"Christ yes!" Her face was screwed up as she strained to reach her orgasm. "Don't let him stop!"

I increased the pace and she came, arching her body in the bed and moaning with pleasure.

Gradually her breathing slowed and she kissed me, licking my face as her hand worked its way back to my still rigid cock.

I put my arm around her, squeezing her breasts hard against my chest.

"I think she'd reward Alan by sucking his cock, don't you?"

She chuckled.

"She might."

"Shall I write that in?"

"Okay!"

She pulled the sheet away and slithered down the bed. I lay back and closed my eyes as her tongue travelled up and down my cock and then groaned with pleasure as she took it in her mouth and began to suck. I was beginning to lose myself in the sensation when she stopped and as I opened my mouth to protest her lips clamped on mine. She forced her tongue into my mouth and kissed me hard, then rolled on to her back and pulled me on top of her.

"I'm still so horny, sweetheart," she whispered. "Fuck me, please!"

Her long fingernails ran up and down my back, making me shiver with pleasure as I slid my cock into the hot, velvety flesh. Her muscles gripped me, her legs wrapped around my waist and I thrust hard into her as she pulled my face down to her breasts.

"Suck my tits, baby, please!" She was bucking so wildly it was hard to stay with her and the bedsprings screeched in protest.

Her nails tore my skin. "Harder, harder!"

I slammed into her, sucked her nipples then ground my lips on hers and sucked her tongue into my mouth.

Her nails clawed my back as she came, her muscles gripping my cock and she urged me on, her body arching up to meet my thrusts as she came again and then again. I could no longer hold back and spurted frantically inside her as she came yet again and we collapsed together on the sweat-soaked sheets.

After what seemed a very long time I looked down into her dark brown eyes.

"Christ," I gasped, "that's one of the best fucks I've ever had! What brought that on?"

She grinned wickedly. "I thought you might write me out of the plot," she said. "I wanted us both to come at least once more before that happened."

She bounced out of bed and went across to the bathroom door, then looked back.

"But as I'm still here, as a critic, I think Alan would enjoy licking the good old librarian's pussy until she comes, don't you? Why don't you write that in?"

"Okay."

The bathroom door closed behind her.

"And I think the librarian would enjoy being tied to the bed with velvet cord and tickled until she begged for mercy," I murmured to myself. "I might write that in …"

Beautiful Sin
by Penelope Friday

It was the ultimate sin.

'The wrong path of love'. 'A wicked perversion'. Catherine knew it had been called both of those things; knew, too, that in a country where King George himself was in a mental institution, it would be easy enough for two ordinary girls to be sent to a hospital for the insane because of their forbidden love affair. And yet – and yet – it was acceptable, even expected, for letters between friends to hold passionate declarations of faithfulness and adoration. Catherine had seen lines from an epistle of her sister Maria to her latest 'best friend': effusive and overblown, they had read, "Every hour seems a day without you, dearest Isobel. I miss my beloved friend with all my heart." Catherine could write no such flowing lines. Her letters were plain yet heartfelt; the most expansive comment her final adieu to Elizabeth – "I miss you greatly." Elizabeth knew all the emotion that was contained in that simple sentence.

But Maria had positively scolded Catherine for her cold reception of Elizabeth that morning. The two girls' eyes had met, they had exchanged smiles. For a couple of precious seconds they had clasped each other's hands.

"Catherine!" Lizzie had exclaimed, the word a caress.

Catherine had felt her throat contract with love as she

heard the beloved voice again.

"It is good to have you here," was all that she could trust herself to say.

How Maria had been indignant! She had taken over the welcome herself, feeling that Catherine had not done justice to the situation.

"Elizabeth, how lovely it is to see you again. How was the journey? Was your carriage comfortable? We are so pleased you were able to visit!"

Later, when Elizabeth was upstairs, unpacking her band boxes, Maria had turned upon Catherine.

"Honestly, Catherine! You have been parted from your oldest friend for more than a month, and yet all you can say is that it is good to have her to stay? How cold you are! I should be ashamed to have nothing warmer to say to the least of my friends!"

Catherine had bowed her head and agreed that she was indeed a sad case; but if Maria had seen her that night, she would not have called her cold – although she would, no doubt, have been scandalised further...

The household was all in bed as Catherine slipped down the corridor to Elizabeth's room and knocked softly on her door. Elizabeth had let her in, and with the door closed and locked behind them, Elizabeth had opened her arms and Catherine had nestled into them, tears in her eyes.

"Lizzie. My darling."

The kisses were clumsy and fumbling at first: too urgent to be gentle or well placed. Catherine kissed Elizabeth's mouth; her cheek; her neck; her ear. Anywhere that she could place her lips she did.

"Kate, oh Kate!" And Lizzie – the only person in the world to call Catherine by that name – was half-laughing at her lover's urgency as she touched Catherine's hair and face as if ascertaining that she was indeed real. "Tears, darling? I thought Catherine never cried."

"Catherine doesn't," Catherine responded, her head resting on Elizabeth's shoulder. "Kate does. Oh, Lizzie, it's been so long."

"I know."

And the two girls looked at each other with tragic eyes, for they knew these partings were likely to get longer as they aged. At twenty, their families were already beginning to show anxiety that neither had married.

"Forget I said it," urged Catherine, kissing Elizabeth again. "We have tonight. Don't let's look any further ahead. Tonight…" She drew a deep trembling breath… "Tonight is ours alone."

She leaned back from Elizabeth, her hands on Lizzie's arms, and looked fully at her beloved for the first time. She had not dared do so in public for fear her love would show too plainly. Her love and her desire.

The long dress suited Elizabeth, with the puffed sleeves that were all the rage at the moment. The figured muslin was a simple enough material, but Catherine's breath caught once more when she saw what it hinted of Lizzie's figure. Her heart beat faster at the thought of watching – of, perhaps, helping – her to undress. All the underclothes she despised so much on herself became layers of promise and temptation when she stripped them from Elizabeth. Lizzie wore clothes with an unconsciously sensual air: Catherine had seen men notice it appreciatively before; had seen, indeed, her brother's admiring glances that very evening. "She's mine," she had wanted to hiss, a raging tiger in protection of her own. But now… now was the moment to claim her love.

"You look fierce," murmured Elizabeth, reaching out and pulling the pins from Catherine's hair so that the soft brown locks hung in loose waves around her face. "Do you feel fierce?"

"Only if you want me to be," and Catherine softened immediately as she held Lizzie tight against her, Lizzie's round, lush breasts pressing into her own. "Oh, Lizzie!

And they were kissing once more, the first desperate need quenched and leaving room for variety; a couple of quick teasing pecks followed by a long, deep embrace that left both girls trembling with the force of their mutual desire.

"Maria was shocked by your cool welcome," Lizzie said laughingly as she led Catherine to the bed and sat beside her.

"She raged at me whilst you unpacked," Catherine admitted. Her arm was around Lizzie as if she could not bear to stop touching her, even for a second. "I dared not say anything then, sweetheart, but, you know… don't you?" Catherine sounded unusually anxious, fearful that the month's absence might have brought deeper rifts than the simple agony of being parted.

Elizabeth pressed her beloved down onto the bed, one hand either side of her face as she lay on top of her.

"Silly Kate, to doubt me a second," she chided, kissing Catherine's forehead and then her lips. "Let me show you how I've missed you."

And Lizzie's kisses had a tenderness and warmth that spread through Catherine's body as she responded. It was as if part of Catherine had been buried, needing Elizabeth's touch to reawaken it; and as Catherine returned the kisses, her hands reacquainted themselves with Elizabeth's body, roaming over her back and through the blonde curls of the girl she loved.

"Yes, Kate – yes!" Lizzie whispered, her breath hot on Catherine's cheek.

Catherine was fumbling with the fastenings at the back of Elizabeth's dress, fingers all thumbs as she struggled. Lizzie giggled at her impatience and pulled away, standing up and leaving Catherine lying alone on the bed.

"Shall I show you how?" she teased, quick neat fingers undoing the clasps and allowing her dress to fall to the floor at her feet.

The look in Catherine's eyes showed her feelings; the faint pink flush on her cheeks her arousal.

"You're beautiful, Lizzie," she said, as she had said so many times before, pushing herself up on one elbow at the edge of the bed.

"Only to you;" and Lizzie was kneeling by her side, pressing kisses up her arm.

The petticoat and chemise still hid more than they showed; and Catherine, her senses aroused, wanted more.

"May I help?"

"I told the maid that she need not help me undress," Elizabeth said encouragingly.

"I told mine not to wait up," Catherine replied. "Elizabeth…"

She sat up as Lizzie discarded the petticoat on the floor. Elizabeth stood in front of her dressed only in stays, a short shift and stockings. Elizabeth bent to untie her garters, and the stockings puddled around her feet, where she kicked them off deliberately as she straightened. Catherine's hands trembled towards the lacings on Lizzie's corset. She worked slowly, fingers caressing each inch of Elizabeth as she exposed the thin chemise that was all that was left as a barrier between her hands and Lizzie's skin; her eyes fixed always on Elizabeth's face, enjoying her lover's pleasure as much as her own. The corset fell away, and then, in one leisurely motion, the chemise was pushed over Lizzie's head; and Catherine caught her breath at the perfection facing her, eyes searching for the beauty spot that only she knew – yes, *there*, beneath her lover's breast. Then she moved her head to take a rosy-peaked nipple into her mouth. Her tongue flicked and teased across the sensitive tip, her teeth grazing with the utmost gentleness. Elizabeth gasped, and moaned, and gasped again; one hand on the back of Catherine's head, the other slipping over her lover's shoulder and down inside her dress, fingertips playing on her back.

The smell of Elizabeth was so familiar, and yet so potent; Catherine felt almost dizzy at their closeness. She wanted to bury her head in Lizzie's bosom, breathing her in with every breath. The curves, the soft, warm curves of Elizabeth's figure. Female, like her own; and yet so very different to her own body. Lizzie was rounded where Catherine was angular; abundant where Catherine was sparse; plump and alluring, not thin and lanky as Catherine knew herself to be. And yet…

"You undress," urged Elizabeth. "I want to see you."

And Lizzie's hands were unfastening Catherine's dress with a compulsion equal to Catherine's own: to Lizzie, Catherine's sallow skin was the most exquisite in the world. Catherine gave a little whine of frustration as the hated layers of undergarments were exposed.

"Too many clothes," she plainted fretfully.

And Elizabeth dragged off her petticoat, which rustled sulkily as it dropped from her body. Lizzie's fingers were already fighting the stay laces. The time for slowness had passed; they were both too impatient, too frustrated, too *needy*. Skin against skin against skin; the chemise was ruthlessly tugged away and Lizzie collapsed onto the bed with Catherine, legs tangling suggestively; hands pulling in Catherine's hair; mouth warm and wet on her neck. Catherine arched her back, pushing her small, high breasts against Elizabeth, moaning at the delicious friction.

"Kate – *Kate*!"

Lizzie was humming a continuous note of pleasure against Catherine's neck, the sound sending shivers through her. Catherine ran desperate, longing hands down Elizabeth's back, cupping her bottom and pulling her closer, always closer.

"I want all of you – all of you," she murmured huskily, rubbing up against Lizzie in every possible place.

There was a thin sheen of sweat covering both girls, and

their bodies slid against each other. Catherine dug her nails into Lizzie, marking her in places no one else would ever see; and Lizzie bucked against her as the pleasure-pain hit. Then Catherine's hand moved round between them, slipping between Elizabeth's thighs and shifting back and forth, feeling the dampness within and knowing without words what Lizzie liked. Her fingers teased and twisted, finding the spots that pleased Elizabeth most; and Elizabeth squirmed in pleasure, her breathing accelerating, her hands still twisted through Catherine's hair.

"There – oh yes, darling."

The words were mumbled against Catherine's cheek as Lizzie gave herself up to her lover. Catherine could taste the saltiness of Elizabeth's skin, hear and feel her fevered breath on the side of her face. Lizzie was moaning softly as Catherine stroked her body with one hand, her other still playing in the warm depths between her legs. Elizabeth's hands clutched and moved, until in one moment she caught fire, her entire body pulsing as she orgasmed. For a minute she lay, panting, blonde hair falling across Catherine's breasts, clinging to Catherine as if she couldn't bear to let go. Catherine wondered, for one heart-stopping second, how many times they would ever do this again. But Elizabeth spoke, and the world receded once more.

"And now, Kate, let me pleasure you…"

Lizzie had lifted herself onto an elbow and was gazing devotedly at Catherine's body; at the breasts with their small coffee-coloured nipples, down to the thatch of light brown curls that lay at the apex of her thighs. Catherine's body tingled at the look, at the promise it held.

"Lizzie?" she begged, as Elizabeth seemed lost in her admiration.

Elizabeth laughed.

"My impatient one!" she teased. "What do you want, Kate?"

Catherine's hands were reaching out to Elizabeth again,

to pull her closer once more, but Lizzie leaned back out of range.

"Please?"

"I will, darling," promised Lizzie.

She drew one hand down the length of Catherine's body, stroking her with a light, tantalizing touch. She laughed again at the expression on Catherine's face.

"You want more?"

"Mmm."

Catherine's bottom lip was gripped between her teeth, her head arced back to show her long smooth neck. It had been so long, so long...

Elizabeth knelt over her and pressed a kiss to her lips. Her hands were on Catherine's breasts, rolling and kneading them between her fingers.

"That's nice?"

Catherine made a noise of appreciation, deep in her throat, and Lizzie smiled lovingly at her.

"What if I do this?" she asked, one hand reaching down further, tickling the light curls between Catherine's legs.

It was wonderful and terrible – too much and yet not enough. Catherine thrust up towards Elizabeth's hand, and Elizabeth allowed her fingers to wander lower, sliding one, then two fingers inside her lover.

"Yes..."

The word was gasped as Catherine's hands reached up to touch Lizzie, pulling down on her shoulders to keep herself steady. The sweat shimmered on her body, pooling between her breasts. She wanted more – more – *there*. Shamelessly, she encouraged Elizabeth, her whispered words becoming steadily more incoherent as she came closer to the brink. Then – *ah* – Lizzie's mouth was on her breast, her fingers never ceasing to move inside her; and Catherine climaxed; the world shattering, transforming, to be made anew more perfect than before.

Sated, the two girls lay together on the bed, arms

clasping each other closely, exchanging light kisses of thanks and happiness; of warmth, of caring, of *love*.

If it was sin, it was a beautiful sin.

The Spying Game
by Roz MacLeod

'Karl Smith.' Control lit a small cigar. I stared at the projector screen. I saw a sturdy man, unruly dark hair, classical profile. Not bad looking for a scientist. He wore a long, belted raincoat and carried a newspaper tucked under his arm.

'His mother's Russian,' Control continued, puffing at her cigar. 'Just your type, Sandi.'

I recalled my encounter with Oblonsky, a top communist agent. I had been the means of Oblonsky's downfall. Life imprisonment with no chance of an exchange.

Control fastened the top button of her pinstriped jacket, rose to her feet and switched on the light.

'Bearing in mind your excellent impersonation of a whore, I would like you to role-play your way into Dr Smith's affections. He's working for us, but we are suspicious about his links with Moscow Centre.'

'A double agent?'

'Exactly.'

'Same as before?' I'd had such fun pretending to be a high class prostitute.

'Not entirely. Dr Smith will be attending a scientific conference at Pensley Manor at the weekend. He's giving a lecture.'

'I know nothing about science,' I protested.

'You don't need to. You'll be attending,' she stroked her tie, 'as the cabaret – one of the dancing girls.'

Since my parents had died at the hands of the Nazis, I was more than willing to play the game and do anything keep my country free and safe from tyrants. I stood, discarded my swing jacket and postured in my apricot blouse, my pencil skirt and red beret.

'What sort of dancing?' I began to gyrate my pelvis. Control would appreciate a private show.

She pressed a button under her desk and narrowed her wicked eyes. 'Striptease, Sandi.'

I giggled and undid buttons on my blouse. My breasts swung forward, slipping out of their silk camisole. I was not wearing a brassiere, so my nipples bounced freely in front of Control's eager face. I teased her, spinning round, unzipping my skirt, which slithered to the floor.

Control's cheeks went red. Her pants must be wet, I thought, my forefinger pressing my moist clitoris under my French knickers. It excited me to have such power over my boss. I let my knickers fall in a slinky movement. I stroked my auburn fur and invited her to put her hands right there.

Her plump fingers tugged at my pussy, she found my hole and stirred in and around. My juices ran down my legs. I sat astride her, my wetness seeping into her trousers. Her fingers moved ever quicker, massaging my clit to an exquisite agony.

I gripped her shoulders and convulsed so hard my beret fell off.

'Good enough?' I climbed from her soggy lap and bent down to pick up my beret and presenting her with my bare bum.

She slapped me on my cheeks. I wiggled about for more, but she didn't oblige.

'I'll let you know when I've watched your performance again this evening, Sandi.'

I'll say one thing for Control. She's thorough.

I must have passed Control's test, because a couple of days later I received my invitation to the Manor.

I climbed out of the taxi, carrying my weekend holdall. Pensley Manor rose before me, impressively large in the early evening light. The warm brick build, with its lattice windows, the wrought iron balconies, the glow of reception, filled me with wonder and delight. Above all, soared the ancient turreted clock tower, its point reaching high into the clouds as if it went on for ever.

I signed in and was taken to my room. I studied my invitation card. *'Reggie's Red Ravers – modern dance – adults only.'* I grinned as I looked at my reflection in the long mirror on the wall. So that's why Control had chosen me. Titian hair, green eyes, red pussy. *Au naturelle.* 'God bless you, Dad,' I said to myself.

I heard a knock at my door. A ginger haired girl smiled at me. She wore shocking pink lipstick and a salmon satin dressing gown with a big sash at her waist.

'Sandi? I'm Marigold. We've got a rehearsal. Ready?'

'Anytime.' I started taking out the costume Wardrobe had given me on Control's orders.

'Don't bother with that,' Marigold said. 'Our leader wants us to do it naked. So he can see how we move unrestricted-like.'

I swallowed. 'I don't have a dressing gown with me.'

'Just come downstairs in your birthday suit, then. None of the delegates will arrive before dinner.'

'Very well.' I pulled off my blouse and skirt, then my frilly knickers.

'Slim, hourglass figure,' Marigold said. I could see she envied me.

I ran down the maroon carpeted stairway, enjoying the freedom of moving my limbs without restraints. At the bottom stood a statue of the founder of Pensley. Clad in a long robe like an ancient Roman. I stopped, stroked the cool

87

marble and rubbed up against him like a cat. Marigold laughed.

'For luck,' I said, my vagina already twitching from anticipation. I slide a finger in my honeyed hole.

'You'll be a lot hornier when we get going,' Marigold said, her gown slipping from her shoulders. She pointed to her ginger pussy.

'Blokes go mad for this,' she said. I could see it wasn't her natural colour, but I didn't say anything out of politeness. Her skin was far too dark, whereas mine is ivory pale. She was bigger boned than me, but curvaceous enough, the aureoles on her breasts dark. I leant towards her and pinched her nipples. She returned the compliment, her fingers sliding under my swellings. Then she bent down and sucked my breasts, first the left, then the right. I moaned with pleasure.

She let me go, her breath panting.

'Later?'

I nodded. I didn't think I'd have time, but I rarely turned down an opportunity.

I followed Marigold into the hall. Assembled at the summit were the other four red-headed girls who made up the troop of '*Red Ravers*'. Undressed and ready to go. In front of them sat a middle-aged man, a bald patch at the back of his head, his hand resting on a gold-handled cane.

'Reg,' Marigold whispered.

We took our places in the line of dancers. Somebody switched on the music. Reg raised his cane. 'Now,' he shouted, 'remember, from the top to the bottom.'

I copied the others. He meant we had to shake our top half, before wiggling our belly and our hips. It was quite easy. Two of the girls had waist length hair, so they made much play of this – tossing it back, twirling round their nipples, catching it in their teeth.

The music increased in volume and quickness. We gyrated as fast as possible. Marigold winked at me and I started giggling. She moved nearer to my body. I pressed my pelvis against hers. Now we were moving together, breast against breast, pussy against pussy. The wetness flowed from my labia and down my thighs.

The music slowed, but we continued nuzzling each other.

'Nice,' Reg said. 'Good girls.'

'He might give us a bonus', Marigold murmured in my ear. She cupped a hand round my bum and fingered my anus. I groaned in delight. 'Not too loud,' she said.

Reggie's expression was full of admiration. 'You two gotta lot of imagination, I must say.'

In answer, I raised one of my legs for Marigold to lick my vagina. My back arched, I couldn't help myself, my body jolted, I writhed and came in flood of orgasm. The other girls clapped. Reggie got to his feet, his face shining, the bulge in his striped trousers like a tent pole.

'Well done. Best ever.' He glanced at his watch. 'Do it again tonight.'

'We will,' I said, looking forward to it. At the same time, I wondered whether he knew I was here for another job really. Control never tells us. Except she gives us a phrase which helps.

'Will the Earl of Pensley be dining tonight?'

Reg looked confused. 'Oh, I don't think so.'

It was the wrong answer.

Back in my room, I showered and put on my costume. Three silver stars. I stuck two on my nipples. The third to cover my private parts, except it wasn't big enough. I fixed it low on my fur. I lifted my arms and donned my emerald top, loose and open to the waist. It hung just above my cunt star. Heavens, I'd forgotten to bring the silk trousers! I searched desperately in my holdall, finally fixing on my amber necklace. I wound the glowing beads round my waist three times and wriggled until they rested over my thighs, meeting the silver star. Very pretty, I decided. I turned round and thrust out the creamy cheeks of my bare bottom.

'Fuck you.' Marigold stood at my unlocked door.

I grinned. Evidently, she had forgotten her top, because her full breasts swung freely, with only the stars covering.

'Thought I'd get in the mood.' She cupped her mounds and danced, twirling her hips in their Turkish pants. I slapped her on the bum and she returned the favour. My clit trembled.

'Wait for it,' I warned. 'We don't want to go off the boil too soon.'

'I'm never off the boil,' she replied. 'And neither are you, are you?'

I followed her into the corridor. 'Will the Earl of Pensley be dining tonight?'

'Who?'

The wrong answer.

We trooped into the splendid dining room. Chandeliers hung at regular intervals over the tables, crystal lights like candles on a huge birthday cake. The mass of delegates swam before my eyes. Where was Karl? I couldn't ask them all about the Earl of Pensley.

Our music started. I took Marigold's hand. Round and round we danced, faster and faster, and at each new movement, the girls removed items of their clothing, lastly, the stars. The delegates clapped and shouted, egging us on. Marigold pushed towards me, her fingers rubbing my clit, then in and out of my hot, wet, twitching quim. I began to thrash about, we collapsed onto the floor. She put her head down, I raised my legs and she sucked my pussy. My body spasmed and I came with a crashing orgasm, my necklace splitting apart, the beads rolling towards the delegates.

'Me, too,' Marigold squealed. I pulled her towards me, stroking her clit with one hand and squeezing her teats with the other. I put her breasts in my mouth and licked and pinched her nipples. Another one of the *Reds* danced up behind, caressed her thighs and stuck her finger up Marigold's bottom. And another girl kissed her lips, her tongue forging towards the back of Marigold's throat. A third ran her silver star down the length of Marigold's body, then licked her ginger pussy, tongue grooving into her juicy hole. Marigold's limbs convulsed. We all shouted to thunderous applause from the audience.

Everyone was smiling and laughing. How good it felt to bring so much happiness to so many! Reg bowed and waved to the audience, pointing at us and clapping his hands at our performance.

He presented us all with bouquets. Mine was russet chrysanthemums, my favourite flower. I pressed it to my breasts and saw the note nestling in the blooms. *'With love from the Earl of Pensley.'* I glanced into the room – and caught the eye of tall, dark haired man. Karl Smith. He held up a handful of amber beads.

By now I was hungry for cock. It's all very well playing with the girls, and I'm sure Control likes me to have a good time, but there's nothing like a huge cock to round off the day. Preferable Karl Smith's cock. I had so little time to get to know him and discover if he had links with Moscow Centre.

In my room, I squeezed into my basque. The lace at the top barely hid my nipples and my breasts stuck out like they were begging to be held. Would that be enough to snare Karl? Like Oblonsky? I powdered my skin and painted my teats lipstick crimson. The black basque contrasted against my lily white skin. The full skirt shone a brilliant sapphire, and my stiletto heels clicked down the passage towards the dining room. I wore no knickers, just a suspender belt to hold up my black silk stockings.

By now, the delegates were very merry with pre-dinner drinks. I sauntered into the room carrying my velvet evening purse. They welcomed me with cat calls. I grinned and searched for Karl. A hand grasped my waist. I turned, my breasts spilling out. Karl pulled me close and my nipples grazed his business suit.

'Let it all hang out,' he said, bending over and taking my nipple in his mouth.

'The Earl of Pensley …' I began.

'…is dining tonight and requests your company,' he continued, licking my darkening aureole and making my crimson nipples swell and harden.

I breathed a sigh of relief. From now on my path was clear.

'Over here.' He led me to a table by one of the wall tapestries. We sat down. Karl pressed his thigh against mine.

'Tell me why you're here. Good show, by the way. Is that what they teach you at London Centre?'

I smiled, proudly. 'Most of it I picked up myself. I'm Sandi. Control asked me to look after you.'

His handsome face crinkled into a frown.

'Why?'

I leant towards him, my bare leg brushing his trousers. He moved his hand under my skirt, fondled my knee, stroked his fingers up my thigh towards my cunt.

'That's nice.' I opened my legs as wide as possible.

Karl renewed his pressure on my pussy. He fingered open my labia and began rubbing my clit. My stomach contracted. I caught my breath.

'Other people,' I warned, as a couple of delegates sat down at our table.

He pulled his finger from my hole and licked it.

'Juicy pussy – *pussy my love, what a beautiful pussy you are* …' I smelt his masculine scent as he put his arm round my bare shoulders and pushed down my basque at the back. My breasts danced free for all to see.

I swallowed a glass of cold white wine to cool my

senses. The whole of my lower body felt on fire. I ached for cock to slide into me, to fill me completely. I glanced at the protuberance in Karl's crotch. He looked big, long too, and raring to fuck me. Under the table I fumbled at his trousers and glided my hand into the slit between the buttons. He jerked. I held on tight. His mouth opened, his cheeks reddened, his breath came in short bursts. I took pity on him and let go his stiff.

Just as well, because our first course was served – asparagus soup. Karl poured me another glass of wine.

'Control is very kind to send you, but tell her I can look after myself.'

'It's not that,' I murmured, 'there are other agents here – communists and anarchists who would die to know our nuclear secrets.'

'Does she think I'm going to tell them in my lecture tomorrow?'

'Not at all. She believes they may kidnap you and force you to tell them.' This was the story Control had asked me to convey to Karl. 'So I am to sleep with you tonight in case they try to break in. Don't worry – I have been schooled in martial arts.'

He seemed surprised. 'Will you show me?'

'I will.'

We galloped through our roast chicken and vegetables.

'Can we have the strawberries and cream served in your room?' I asked.

He snapped his fingers and gave the order.

We left the dining room, Karl carrying another bottle of wine, and hurried upstairs towards his room.

'Take off all your clothes,' I commanded. 'I prefer to work in the nude.'

He removed his suit, his shirt and tie, his underclothes. I gazed at his penis, riding hard and high. His clear blue eyes smiled at me. He had such an open expression I couldn't imagine him being a double agent. Had Control been right?

I let fall my skirt and stood before him in my basque, black stockings and stilettos. He came up to me and unlaced my front.

'Beautiful,' he said, his hands caressing my shoulders, my stomach, my hips. He undid my suspender belt. Then he eased off my stockings, stroking the curves of my calves, the hollows of my ankles. As he bent over, I slid my fingers towards his anus and played with his hole. What a perfect butt! I moved my hand over his slim hips and up to his muscular shoulders. His skin was pale coffee, an all-over tan.

With an effort I stepped back. 'Try to assault me.' I rooted my body and got into the '*ward off*' position.

He ran towards me, grabbed my arm and I threw him back against the bed.

'Blimey,' he said.

'Now from behind.'

He tried again, and I flung him to the carpet.

'Ouch!'

'Tie me up,' I said, 'and have another go.'

Karl undid the leather straps from his case and fastened my wrists to the bed head.

'You can't get out of that.' He bent over me in a threatening movement, I drew up my legs and kicked him in the stomach. He gasped, although I deliberately hadn't hit him hard.

'What about if I tie your ankles, too?'

'Try it,' I pushed the soles of my feet into his face as he endeavoured to do so. At length he had to give up, taking my toes and kissing them.

I squirmed with delight and spread-eagled my legs so he had the best view of my cunt. Combat always turns me on.

Karl's cock thickened. He leant down and sucked my pussy, tonguing right into my slippery hole, coming up for air, then pushing his head down again, his dark curly hair between my legs. My flesh tingled, my clitoris swelled. He

94

found my nub and pinched it between his lips. My stomach contracted – oh, this pleasure could go on for ever!

He reached up and undid the straps round my wrists. Freed, I stroked his hair, pressing him down. I released the pressure, he came up for air, his face smeared with my honey. I licked it off. He bent his knees, came further up the bed and presented me with his bulbous member. I licked all round the head, down the shaft and ran my tongue towards his heavy balls, taking each tenderly in my mouth. He groaned as I found his G spot in front of his anus. I spent some time running my tongue all over this vulnerable area and he let out little gasps of delight.

'Don't forget the strawberries,' I murmured.

Obediently, he fetched over a handful and rubbed them on my breasts. The juice trickled like rivulets down my body and he licked my skin. He shoved another half dozen up my cunt and began to eat, greedily.

But I wanted more. I couldn't hold on much longer, and neither, I guessed, could he.

The last of the strawberries consumed, I lifted my legs over his shoulders. With a gasp of excitement, he thrust his cock into my cunt. It felt so good. He began to move inside me, I clenched my muscles to hold him more tightly. He plunged in further, pumping into my hungry cunt. He thrust in and out, rubbing my clit to distraction.

'I'm coming!' I cried.

'So am I!'

We climaxed together, waves of ecstasy filling my body like vibrant colours and transporting me to a land where everything was so glorious I could have cried.

Panting, we lay close beside each other on the bed. It was an effort to say what I had to say.

'Wonderful, Karl, but I'm worried about my wrists.'

Karl jumped up, his face full of concern. 'They're a bit red, but Sandi, you said you were okay …'

'I know, sweetie, but would you be kind enough to fetch

me my first aid kit. It's in my room – number five on the ground floor.' I leant over to my purse and extracted the key. I laughed. 'Put on your underpants first.'

'I won't be long, darling – I'm so sorry.' He raised my wrists and kissed them. 'Soon be better.'

I waited until I heard his footsteps fade. I sat up and opened his case, now strapless and easy to unlock. Inside were several books, folders marked '*Top Secret*' and wads of paper. Quickly, I opened the folders. Mathematical formulae which meant nothing to me, but words which did. My knowledge of Russian is limited, but I saw enough to realise Karl's top secret formulae had been written with the Ruskies in mind. Sadly, I recognised Control had told me the truth. Karl was indeed a traitor. And it was my job to expose him.

I folded one of the sheets of paper and stuck in the my suspender belt. It nestled against my satisfied pussy. I pulled on my skirt before Karl returned. He carried my kit containing Vaseline. It seemed a shame to waste the ointment, particularly as I would never see Karl again.

I smeared the cream on my wrists. 'Do you fancy – a touch of *sodom?* The ultimate sin?'

'Would you like that, Sandi?'

'I sure would.' At my words, his erection heaved into life again, bulging from his pants like the forceful member it was.

I crouched on the bed, my bum raised high. Karl anointed my anus with Vaseline and gently pressed his way in.

'Harder,' I encouraged him.

'I don't want to hurt you.'

'You won't.' What a pity I worked for London Centre. If only I had been an ordinary girl, like Marigold perhaps, enjoying a night of pleasure.

As he pressed in, I climaxed again. Karl cried out, too.

'Brilliant. I've always wanted to do that to a girl.'

'I've always wanted a man to do it to me,' I confessed. 'We're both virgin anus fuckers.'

'Love you and leave you, Karl.' I sighed. He was such a lovely man. 'I have to go. Things to do.'

Karl looked so crestfallen. I raised my arms and kissed his mouth. His tongue found the back of my throat. Oh, how I should miss him!

I lowered my voice. Would he take the hint and escape?

'The Earl of Pensley travels abroad – I believe the best amber's found in Moscow.' I picked up my loose beads and departed.

'Well done, Sandi. Another job completed.'

My heart raced. Control swivelled in her chair. 'Once you'd left Dr Smith's room, we barged in and took him.'

A sliver of ice ran down my spine.

'No exchange?'

'Not this time. Dr Smith's too important. He'll be settling into his flat off Red Square by now.'

'What d'you mean?'

She heaved her shoulders.

'Karl's continuing his work for Moscow Centre – but he's employed by us at the same time.'

'He's still a double agent?'

'Yes – playing the game in Moscow, instead of London.'

'So – they believe he's one of theirs, whereas, he isn't?'

'Absolutely.'

I took a deep breath. 'Can we trust him?'

Control didn't answer.

'Do you think we'll ever be friends with the communists?' I asked.

'Give it six years,' she replied. 'New friends, new enemies. By the way, what was all that about amber beads in Moscow?'

'I lost my necklace dancing,' I said, without changing my expression.

She nodded. 'Good show, Sandi. Bugged the room, naturally. Enjoyed listening. Virgin anus fuckers, my arse! Clever girl.'

I collected my bonus. Six years might be a long time to be without amber beads, but who knows, I might just wait.

Eat Me
by Elizabeth Cage

She was right. The bloke was urinating against the wall in the alleyway beside the bus station. Quite blatantly, too. The question was, what to do about it. And Joanne knew she had to do something. It wasn't a situation she'd encountered before. Not like telling someone off for trampling on the grass when there was a *No Trespassing* sign.

It was 6.30pm and Joanne had just finished another stressful day at the call centre where she worked in Customer Services. She didn't want any more hassle. She was fed up with dealing with other people's complaints. At this moment all she wanted was to get home to her nice quiet flat and lovingly devour a double chocolate fudge cake.

"Excuse me."

As she spoke, the man glanced over his shoulder at her, not in the least distracted from the task in hand.

"Excuse me," she repeated. "I don't think you should be doing that in a public place."

"Why not?"

She was incredulous. "Why not? Because you're breaking the law."

"Show me the sign, then, that says No Pissing."

For a moment she was taken aback. The man stared at

her, his toffee-brown eyes brazen, and she noticed that his caramel-coloured hair looked soft and freshly washed, and his bronzed complexion reminded her of a crème brulée. She began to feel hungry.

"You shouldn't need a sign. It's obvious."

He studied her curiously, gestured around him to the numerous passers-by who behaved as if it was a normal Friday night occurrence in the rush hour. "Do you see anyone complaining?" he asked.

Now he was getting on her nerves.

He continued cheekily, "Am I inundated with protests? I think not."

They had reached stalemate.

Glaring at him, Joanne noticed that although he was behaving like a lout, he was not dressed like one. In fact, he was smartly attired, with liquorice-black trousers, a creamy white shirt open at the neck and a leather blouson-style jacket the colour of Bournville chocolate. He looked good enough to eat.

Joanne wondered what to do next. Perhaps she should call the police. She was certain he must be committing some kind of criminal offence. Indecent exposure. Or was it gross indecency? Thank goodness her mobile phone was tucked neatly in her shiny handbag. Her fingers encircled it, cradling, ready to dial. And then the strangest thing happened. She was seized by a powerful urge to place her hands elsewhere.

The man noticed with interest where her eyes were straying.

"Do you want to touch it?" he asked.

Appalled at the suggestion, Joanne shook her head vigorously. But the man took her hand and gently placed it over his rapidly stiffening cock. She felt that she should have protested. Instead, she closed her fingers. His circumference and length were indeed impressive, crying out to be touched. She grasped him firmly and began to move her hands up and down.

"Harder," he cried.

Joanne considered the steel rod in her hand. "I don't think you could get much harder," she replied. He groaned.

"Oh, you mean you want me to rub harder?"

Within minutes, the man came loudly. Joanne suddenly wondered about the passers-by. But it was getting dark now, and no-one seemed to notice them.

"Thank you." The man calmly zipped up his flies and smoothed down his shirt.

She nearly replied, "No problem. Think nothing of it." She even considered,

"That will be fifty pounds please." Her head was spinning. She fumbled for a tissue to wipe the stickiness from her hand.

"Thank you," he repeated, kissing her lightly on the forehead and before she could respond his hand was under her stretch-cotton skirt, between her legs, his fingers feather-touching through her mocha tights.

She was vaguely aware of her own murmuring, and surprised at her own excitement. She remembered reading an article somewhere that sex was so much easier with a stranger. And after all, she was hungry. Very hungry.

Carefully, he pulled down her tights. She didn't protest. In fact, she felt almost embarrassed at the creeping wetness that she knew must be visible through her white cotton knickers. Smiling, he pulled the fabric to one side and continued to stroke her clit.

"Relax," he whispered.

But her muscles seemed to be going into involuntary contractions as his thumb pressed softly, increasing the pressure between her legs. She groaned. In response, he teased her with his fingers, playing with her swollen pussy, her juices supplying all the lubrication he needed as he slowly slid a finger inside her. She gasped as tiny electrical impulses were soon transformed into jolts that threatened to consume her aching body. Any self control she was clinging onto soon vanished. She thrust her hips forward, pushing urgently against his hand. He moved his finger in and out of her, and she became aware of the slurping sounds emanating from her pussy, like he was dipping into a pot of honey. Lifting a finger to her lips, he said, "Taste yourself." As she licked the juices dripping from his finger, his tongue joined hers, relishing the taste.

"Good, isn't it?" he breathed. He ran the base of his thumb around her clit, adding to the exquisite sensations that threatened to engulf her completely. She shuddered as the first wave hit her, so powerful he had to slip his other hand around her waist to steady her. But still his fingers continued to stroke and almost before she knew it, she was coming again, gasping with the force of it.

When she was finished he got down on his knees and licked her clean, relishing each mouthful as if it were golden syrup.

"I'm still hungry," he said. "What about you?"

"Ravenous," Joanne replied, still reeling. "We've had the starter – how about the main course?"

"And mustn't forget the dessert," he murmured, pushing back her fitted jacket and caressing her erect nipples through her blouse. He stopped to undo her top button, then the next one, then the next, until the ivory cream lace of her bra was clearly visible. He slid his hand inside, gently squeezing the soft flesh. He closed his eyes, as if savouring the sensation. Joanne wondered how she would feel if someone saw her now. Her work colleagues would be shocked. Her mother would be horrified. But somehow, she didn't care. She was enjoying herself too much. The man opened his eyes and met her gaze. Her cheeks were flushed red, her lips moist and parted invitingly. Taking her hand he said, "Come with me."

"I just did," she sighed.

"I know somewhere close by we can go to."

Amazed at herself, Joanne scooped up her discarded tights and allowed this total stranger to lead her down a quiet side road, away from the traffic and bustling commuters. What was she thinking? Had she forgotten the meaning of the word 'caution'? Five minutes later, they were outside what was clearly an expensive restaurant. She felt suddenly foolish. She hadn't expected him to buy her a meal. When he'd talked about being hungry, she'd imagined he'd meant something else.

"Oh. I thought we were going to......that you wanted to–" she mumbled, blushing.

"And you were right," he replied, grinning.

Then she noticed the restaurant was in darkness, obviously closed.

"We open in two hours," he said, taking a key from his pocket. "Plenty of time."

Joanne hesitated. "What about your boss?"

"I am the boss."

He flicked a switch and the dining area was flooded with light, revealing clusters of neatly dressed bistro tables, draped in white tablecloths, each decorated with a cut glass stem vase containing a lilac freesia. Tasteful modern paintings adorned the white walls. He led her to a quiet alcove at the back of the restaurant.

"This is reserved for couples who prefer some privacy," he explained. Briskly removing the vase and bread basket, he lifted her onto the table. His hands on her knees, he carefully parted her legs, his lips brushing her thighs. Joanne felt her heart pounding. Pushing her skirt up over her hips, he pulled her knickers down and over her ankles.

"I don't think we need these, do we?" he asked grinning.

Joanne shook her head as he dropped them onto the polished wood floor.

"You smell wonderful," he said, burying his face in her neatly trimmed bush of pubic hair. "Quite delicious, in fact."

"Then eat me," she replied.

And he proceeded to run his tongue between the lips of her labia, causing her to gasp with pleasure. She felt warm and wet, her clit already pulsating with anticipation. He sucked her into his mouth, like he was trying to extract the juice from the sweetest orange. As his tongue probed deeper and deeper, she felt her hot pussy enfolding him. Instinctively, her muscles gripped him, sucking in, then relaxing as he tongue-fucked her. Before long, she was coming again.

"Greedy girl," he joked, gazing admiringly as she lay sprawled across the table, her juices spreading over the white tablecloth. "You'll ruin your appetite." She heard him unzipping his trousers. Her pussy still throbbing, Joanne sat up, and came face to face with his erection.

Feeling it would be bad manners not to return the compliment, she licked her lips and began to suck his renewed hardness rather as she would have done her favourite ice cream lolly.

"That feels good," he groaned, as she flicked her tongue over his knob, tracing its smooth length. She teased him for some time before turning her attention to his balls, licking each one in turn, rolling it in her mouth like a giant profiterole. She could feel him trembling, and guessed he was close to coming.

"Not yet," he sighed, pulling away. "I want this to last."

But he couldn't resist her for long.

"Feed me," she demanded and he soon thrust his cock back into her mouth, filling it. He gasped as she deep-throated him before sliding her mouth away, until only the tip of his cock was held tantalisingly between her soft lips. She opened her mouth, releasing him.

"Do you want more?" she asked.

He moaned appreciatively. Once again, she took his cock in her mouth, enveloping it, and began to suck vigorously, squeezing, as if she was trying to milk him dry.

Suddenly, he came in violent spurts, the creamy fluid exploding onto her taste buds like heavenly nectar. There was so much of it, too much to swallow it all. The sticky liquid dribbled down the sides of her mouth. She licked her lips, wanting to lap it up. Waste not, want not.

"My compliments to the chef," Joanne joked, wiping her hand across her mouth. But still she wasn't satisfied. Tonight, she had a big appetite. She wanted more. As he leaned back against the table, still panting, Joanne began to fondle his limp cock, determined to bring it back to life. He laughed, but as she wrapped her hands around it, pumping, he placed his hands over hers, increasing the pressure. It took less time than either of them expected and soon he was stiff once more.

"Very appetising," she observed, pressing her groin against him.

Quickly sensing her mood, he reached into his pocket and produced a pack of strawberry-flavoured condoms.

"Hope you like fruit," he said.

"If it's ripe and juicy," she replied, pushing him down onto the floor. He looked up at her swollen pussy as she stood over him.

"Still hot, I see," he whispered.

Joanne straddled him and carefully lowered herself onto his ramrod cock. She was gaping open, wider than she'd ever been before. He slid inside her, filling her to the hilt in seconds, she was so wet. Closing her eyes, Joanne wrapped her legs around him, clutching him and locking him to her. She alternately gripped and relaxed with her muscles, while he pumped rhythmically.

"Faster," she pleaded.

Gathering speed, he thrust furiously into her, his rampant cock pounding, his balls slapping against her. Finally, her body jerked as waves engulfed her. She felt his cock pulse as her convulsions triggered his orgasm and their bodies shuddered as they came together. They lay panting, their bodies entwined, mutually satiated, waiting for the calm to return.

After a while he said apologetically, "My staff will be arriving shortly."

She reached for her abandoned knickers. "I ought to be getting home," she replied, matter of fact.

"Before you leave, there's something I want to give you," he said, heading for the kitchen. Minutes later he returned.

"I promised you dessert," he said, presenting her with a generous slab of chocolate chip cheesecake. "On the house."

"Thanks, but actually, I'm full up," she replied. Then she added, dipping her finger into the creamy chocolate swirl. "But there are some things a girl simply can't resist."

Vichyssoise
by AstridL

When I was young I loved older men. They gave me gifts and taught me a lot. A lot about balls and sucking cock. And a lot about cooking.

As time went by I developed a penchant for younger men. They let me take the lead and I had them in the palm of my hand, in a manner of speaking. I taught them a little about what pussy liked, and they loved my recipes.

I still enjoyed men, but as I got older I began craving something quite different. My new lover is a vibrant executive and is precociously adept at beating men at their game. Much younger than I, my lover is charming and bright, and adores my recipes. She also has a soft spot for pearls, one of the first things I noticed the day we met in a supermarket down town.

She was after one of those ready-made salads and was leaning across the herbs, blocking my view of the dill and the basil, but exposing the freshest breast with the tightest of brown nipples. Creamy pearls swayed from the slant of her grey power suit, no doubt teasing those nubs to the shape of arousal. Never had a woman's breast moved me, at least never like that, all the way down.

"Have you seen the chives?" I said.

She turned. The movement suddenly pulled me within that unspoken ring of heightened interest, crossing the border from decorum to intimacy. My throat felt hot. It wasn't the first time; it had been happening often lately, but not quite like this. She spun around, back to me, and then turned, a bunch of chives in her hand, held out like a bouquet.

The movement took me by surprise. Bold, it brought me back to the present. "Thank you," I said and then smiled.

"What are you making?"

"It's for Vichyssoise."

"Vichyssoise? You can make that yourself?"

I nodded.

"I'd love to try some."

And I'd love you to do that, I thought. But we were in a supermarket and I didn't know her name.

"My name's Sam. Short for Samantha," she said.

What could I do but answer. "Sophia," I said. And then we shook hands.

I don't know if it was because of the way her hand lingered in mine. Her hand was soft and warm yet felt so strong and it seemed then as if the touch of our hands somehow sealed a sensual pact; and it all seemed so natural. So I invited Sam to come home and watch me prepare the cold soup.

I lost little time in readying the ingredients for the Vichyssoise: the white delicate parts of leek, washed well and slivered; the potatoes peeled and sliced thin; the butter, melted evenly over a low, low heat, that swallowed the leeks which turned gradually golden. The aroma was comforting, almost homey. "Would you like some wine?" I said.

Sam nodded. "Do you mind if I slip off my shoes?"

I poured two glasses from an open bottle of St Emilion. "You can slip out of that jacket as well, if you like. I'll get you a cardigan."

Sam sipped her wine. "I'd like that," she said.

When I came back with the apricot cashmere Sam stood

with her back to me, sans jacket and stirring the leeks in the butter. "Thank you for keeping an eye on the soup," I said.

Sam suddenly turned, the wooden spoon in her right hand. The baroque pearls hung over one breast, just grazing the nipple.

"They're gorgeous," I whispered.

A thick droplet of soup rolled from the spoon.

"Careful," I said as I took the spoon from her hand and laid it down gently in the porcelain spoon rest. "Slip into this." I handed her my favourite cardigan and watched her dress.

She began to button two holes at her midriff and I found myself praying that she would not button much higher. As if reading my mind she just buttoned one more.

"Do we add the potatoes?" she said.

My cheeks felt hot. "We have to add some chicken stock first. Then we slip in the potato slivers."

"I can do it," she said and leant by my arm, affording me a full view of both delicious breasts as she gently shook the potato slices into the unctuous mixture. When it had simmered to a soft texture, I showed her how to puree, pushing, kneading with an antique masher – a gift from a former culinary lover. When the texture was fine, we added milk and pepper and simmered again.

"It smells so good," Sam said.

"Cold soups like to be over-seasoned," I said. "They can take it."

Then we added the cream: I poured as Sam stirred, swirling the cream gently into a soup that before my eyes was metamorphosing from a hearty peasant stock to a luxurious sop of bourgeois decadence. The whole process was starting to transport me from simple arousal to an exciting state of pre-orgasm.

"What about the chives?" Sam said.

Her voice brought me back. I had arranged the chives in a glass. "They'll be chopped and sprinkled all over."

"I want to taste it," she said.

I shook my head. "You'll have to wait."

"Please?"

"It has to chill overnight." I was enjoying being in charge. It was something I relished, even if just once in a while.

"I can't wait," she said. "Unfortunately." And then she stroked a finger down my cheek past my throat and suddenly slipped her hand in my bra and pinched my already taut right nipple. Then, as if a question she had asked had just been answered, she withdrew her hand, cupped my face in her palms and kissed me fully on the lips. Her tongue darted between them. "Can I visit you when I am back in town?" she whispered.

"When will that be?" My voice was hoarse.

"Two weeks. Can I borrow the cardigan?"

I nodded. I had tried hard, but again I was smitten. She loved my food. It always was the way to my core.

Sam comes back regularly. She doesn't have much time, but what she does have is pure quality. Intense. Good to look forward to. It lets me consolidate, take stock. It's better for her and for me. For her, as it lets her get on with her work and lets her get off as she chooses. And I can play with my cooking, indulge my memories and fantasies and look forward to her coming.

Sam brings me gifts when she comes every few weeks. Fragrant oils – vanilla, musk. Sometimes toys, to keep me going until her next visit. Once she brought me a couple of shiny shocking pink balls connected by a pink latex string. A tiny looped stringlet for hooking a finger to ease the balls out hung cheekily from one of them; I couldn't resist fingering it for size.

"Wear them for a few hours daily," Sam said. "They will tone your muscles."

I did. They were smooth, fitted snugly inside me. And

because they were weighted and the little weights moved when I did, I swore that my shocking pink balls also sang. My cunt sang as I walked and I thrilled to the thought that others might hear. I'd walk at home naked and with slow rhythmic movements I'd expose my ripe cunt lips and sweet puckered butthole to the glint of glass in the sunlight coming from a window across the way. I'd sometimes sit facing the long French windows and thrill to the thought of the show I was giving as I twirled and tugged on the string of my balls, rocking my hips and listening to the quiet twang.

But that and another sensation were ones I kept to myself: I didn't tell Sam about the added value of my clit nub fitting just into the little loop handle so that when I walked and rolled my hips to the tune of a rhythmic twang the tiny girdle would keep me going and more importantly, coming. It was quite delectable as she was to see when she withdrew the balls on her next visit. They were covered in cream.

"Mmm, reminds me of something," she said, as she took each ball in her mouth. "I never did get to taste the chilled soup."

"I poured in some cream at the end. Brought it almost to body temperature."

"I've missed you. Wear your pink balls to dinner."

I wanted nothing better than that. I was empty and nicely throbbing and longed to be filled again, specially with her there. It was summer time. Thick creamy cold soup with a smattering of chives would be just the thing. The bistro down the street was open and served Vichyssoise.

At dinner we sat side by side and as we were about to sip from our wine she asked me: "Are you wearing your balls?" I smiled and then nodded. "Good," she said. "And I have a new gift." Sam passed me a little cloth packet. Grey pearl earrings. Perfectly baroque. I pierced them through my lobes and Sam stuck her tongue in my ear, swirling it around to finish with a lap over the dark pearly nub.

We walked the two blocks back to my apartment. I could hear the subtle ding of the pink balls within me. Sam had a hand down the back of my pants and was caressing my crack. "Stick your butt out a bit as you walk," she whispered and licked my earlobe, sucking imperceptibly on my pearl. I did as I was told; the balls inside me moved deliciously, and as I tensed my muscles the little girdle pulled on my clitoris. Her middle finger was stroking the puckered skin of my arse. I loved the sensation, but I was not going to come in the middle of the street. That would be going too far, far too soon. "Sam!"

Sam withdrew her hand and laughed. "I have something else," she said. "But wait till we're comfortable."

Out on the balcony in the moonlight she undressed me. I wondered if my neighbour was watching. Although I couldn't see the glint of his telescope by night I knew he was in for another show. Or was it a she? A friend of Sam's maybe? Checking on me? I laughed. I loved the idea of somebody watching.

"Lie down," Sam said. I did as was told. She played with my nipples and then, as if she couldn't wait any longer, her hand slipped between my thighs and her finger hooked in the little clit girdle. "That's enough now. It's my turn. Hold your breath." She pulled gently and one ball popped out, sulkily almost, and then the other.

I was throbbing. "I'm so wet, Sam."

"I can see that."

The balls were dripping. "It's much thicker this time."

"Crème de la crème. Hotter than Vichyssoise, my darling. Come suck with me," she said. And we each sucked my cream from both of the balls.

"I said I had something special. Close your eyes and lean back," Sam said.

Again I did as told. Suddenly, a delicious cold: caviar,

hard like pearls, but a little irregular. She crammed them into my cunt. The sensation of the shapes and the cold was mind-blowing.

"Open your eyes."

She held a mirror in front of me. Two diamond clasps at the end of a string of pearls the size of hazelnuts hung from my pussy. She pushed and rubbed.

"How does that feel?"

I was exploding. Lights shooting behind my eyes. Creaming.

"You look gorgeous like that. I knew we'd find a special way to share my Tahitian pearls." Then she pulled them slowly from my cunt – each one rubbing the insides of my vagina, running over my clit, against my swollen lips, bringing with the pearls a gush from the sea within me. I had never experienced anything like it. "Sam, I'm ..."

"Ejaculating," she said triumphantly. "Join the club, darling." Then she pulled down her pants and straddled my face. "Suck me dry, baby."

"You know that's impossible, Sam," I said as I burrowed my face between her thighs and began lapping the flow of her thick, warm juices.

"Remind you of something?"

"Mmmm," I said. The cream always comes right at the end, but I swear I could taste a slight tang of chives.

French Connection
by Cathy King

Camping la France. Mandy sighed with relief as the sign loomed up ahead. She could hardly believe she'd made it on her own. Jason had never let her drive abroad and her French was almost non-existent.

Feeling rather pleased with herself, she steered the silver convertible onto a narrow road banded by fields of young green sweetcorn. It was June and the sky was a clear midsummer blue. In a month or two the sun would have bleached it to the shade of stonewashed denim.

She sighed again, this time with pleasure, glad she'd come. Several weeks had passed before she'd accepted that Jason, her husband of five years, had found someone new and wasn't coming back. Drowning in abject misery, her first instinct had been to cancel the camping holiday they'd booked together, but friends had urged her to go, saying a change of scenery was just what she needed.

A tractor trundled towards her, taking up most of the narrow road. She slowed and pulled onto the verge to let it pass. As the tractor closed, she found her eyes drawn to the driver's bronzed and naked torso. His bulging chest muscles gleamed with perspiration. He was gorgeous. He raised a hand in thanks; then, as he drew level, his face broke into a huge smile.

"Oooh, mademoi*selle*! Très belle! Très, trè*s belle*!"

Mandy flushed with pleasure. She was used to male reaction to her large breasts, but the attentions of a sexy Frenchman were far more welcome than those of his British counterparts. Unlike the French, most British males hadn't a clue when it came to sexual technique, including Jason. And since he'd dumped her, Mandy had gone right off British men anyway. They were all the same: a bunch of self-obsessed, two-timing bastards.

The sounds of the tractor's motor and driver's whistles faded away. Mandy adjusted her strappy top and admired her breasts with a grin. Not a scrap of silicone in sight. She put the convertible in gear and pulled away.

The lush farmland ended quite suddenly. The car crested a hill and there were the famed pine forests of the Atlantic coast. They stretched as far as the eye could see, to the north on her right, to the south on her left.

She drove into the deep green coolness, relieved to be out of the late afternoon sun for a while, and pushed her sunglasses up onto her dark, windswept hair. The heady scent of pines hit her with a sudden rush and she inhaled deeply. The salty tang of the Atlantic bit at the back of her throat. She laughed out loud, feeling more alive than she had in years.

The campsite appeared ahead, orange tents peeping through the tree-trunks like shy flowers. She braked beside a tent adorned with a lazily-flapping sign advising *BRITISH CAMPERS REGISTER HERE* and killed the engine.

The silence of the forest was breathtaking, the crashing of Atlantic rollers filtered to a whisper by the imposing pines. The campsite would be a peaceful haven until August, the main attraction of holidaying in June. Most of the few campers currently resident would be French, and on the beach or visiting nearby tourist draws. They'd return later, cars laden with wine from local vineyards, or run up from the beach, happy and laughing, surfboards and brightly-coloured towels wedged beneath sunburnt arms.

The smell of suppers cooking on two-ring hobs would drift through the forest for an hour or so, then everyone would congregate in the bar, drink too much, and make plans for the following day. According to the *Camping la France* brochure, the bar stood at the edge of the forest, overlooking the beach. The sunsets were apparently spectacular.

Mandy climbed from the car and entered the living area of the reception tent. It was like all the other tents she'd seen on French campsites: a small oven with a two-ring hob; a fridge; a well-stocked utensil rack; table and plastic patio chairs. The only difference was that the table was piled high with paperwork and colourful brochures.

A groan came from the zipped sleeping quarters at the back of the tent, followed by the rhythmic squeaking of bedsprings.

"Oh, Teddee," breathed a French girl's voice. "Ted*deee*…"

Mandy grinned. So the courier's name was Teddy. Probably a student on his gap year. She coughed loudly and the bedsprings stopped squeaking.

"Anyone there?" she called mischievously.

The sounds of frantic scrabbling and a zip being fastened reached Mandy's ears. The compartment's own zip fastener whizzed down and a tanned, twenty-something hunk dressed only in denim shorts stepped through and quickly zipped it up again.

"Sorry," breathed the young Adonis, running a hand through his dishevelled dark locks. "I'm Teddy, the British site representative. And you are…?" His eyes firmly fixed on Mandy's breasts, he fumbled ineffectually for a folder on the table.

"Mandy. Mandy Turner."

Teddy forced his gaze upwards, to Mandy's smiling face. "You made good time. I wasn't expecting you for at least another hour."

Mandy's eyes travelled down to the erection straining against Teddy's tight shorts. "So I see," she murmured.

Muffled giggles sounded from the sleeping compartment. Teddy blushed to the roots of his hair and sat down, having finally located the registration form. Mandy sat down opposite him and completed the form, acutely aware that Teddy was far more interested in her breasts than her details. Despite the heat, her nipples began to harden. Teddy was far from unattractive.

"Okay then." Teddy stood up. "I'll show you to your tent if you'd like to follow me."

Despite the embarrassment her early arrival had caused, Mandy noted that Teddy was still hard, his clearly-defined cock angled against his groin. Still, with a French girl in his bed, and Mandy's braless breasts to keep him entertained in the meantime, maybe that wasn't surprising.

She followed him through the trees to the shower and laundry block, and then on to her assigned pitch. He showed her the tent's equipment, and how the oven and hob worked, casting lustful glances at her breasts. Mandy couldn't resist teasing him. She pretended to test the bed, aware of the effect every tantalising bounce of her breasts was having on him.

Teddy licked his lips and moved towards her. He stood in front of her, his stiff cock straining towards the waistband of his shorts. Mandy felt a rush of sticky warmth soak her knickers. She couldn't help herself. She reached up and pulled down his zip a couple of inches, then reached out a tentative finger and touched the purple head of his erection. Teddy gasped and pre-cum welled up from the eye and trickled over Mandy's finger.

She snatched back her hand. What the hell did she think she was doing? If she was going to shag anyone on this holiday, it would be a mature Frenchman, not some fumbling British student.

She stood up abruptly and flashed him a shaky smile.

"Thanks for showing me around, Teddy. You'd better get back to your girlfriend."

Teddy swallowed his disappointment. "Sorry. My fault." His gaze dropped to her breasts again. "It's just that…"

"I know," said Mandy. "You're into big tits."

They both laughed.

"If you need anything, you know where I am," said Teddy, and blushed again, realising how that sounded. "Campsite-related stuff, I mean."

"I know what you mean," laughed Mandy.

"Oh." He paused in the doorway. "I almost forgot – you do know the beach is a nudist beach? For those that want it, I mean. I don't mean you have to strip off if you don't want to." He blushed again.

Mandy nodded. "Yes, I know. It said in the brochure."

"Okay. See you around then."

Mandy watched him stride back through the trees, his bum tight and muscled in his shorts. Time to fetch the car and have a shower.

The car safely parked, Mandy took a change of clothes down to the deserted shower block. As she undressed, she thought of Teddy's cock. Her pussy began to throb again. Hot water cascading off her breasts, Mandy slid her hand down between her legs and began to massage herself with the soapy sponge.

Female voices, speaking rapidly in French, interrupted her journey to orgasm. Two cubicle doors banged closed nearby.

People were beginning to return to the campsite. She decided to go down to the beach. Atlantic beaches were vast, so she was bound to find a private spot.

Back at the tent, she found her beach mat and towel, then headed through the trees, dressed in shorts and bikini top. As she neared the beach, the trees thinned to scrub and she found herself standing on a grassy sand dune in the evening sun, a salt-laden breeze warm on her skin.

The glistening sea heaved and rolled, crashed and foamed. Surfers rode the waves beneath a deep blue sky flecked with wheeling, screeching gulls. Below her, several people, most naked, sun-bathed or sat watching the surfers. But most were collecting their belongings, preparing to return to the campsite for supper. The vast expanse of sand to her left and right was practically deserted.

Mandy set off along the top of the dune to her left, slipping and sliding in the soft, warm sand, until she reached a hollow that was slightly exposed to the seaward side. She unrolled her mat, laid it on the sand, and covered it with her towel. Seconds later, her shorts and bikini were off and laid in a neat pile at one end of the towel; a makeshift pillow for later. Totally naked, she stood and faced the sea, her heart and pussy pumping with excitement. Two figures strolled along the shoreline in the distance.

A trickle of sweat rolled from beneath Mandy's left breast. She'd never swum naked before, and the sea looked cool and inviting and as wild as she felt. With a whoop of joy, she ran, turned on further by the feel of her swinging, bouncing breasts. She waded into the receding sea until it reached the tops of her thighs. Slowly, she lowered her buttocks and pussy into the cold water and gasped with pleasure as it swirled around her labia. Another wave began to form. Laughing, she turned and waded back to the shore, watching over her shoulder as the wall of water came towards her. She threw herself down in the ankle-deep water at the shoreline and waited. The wave crashed several feet in front of her. Mandy opened her legs and the boiling, foaming water rushed towards her, then over and inside her. She lay back, feeling the tug of the receding wave as the sea reclaimed it, shivering deliciously in the lowering sun. Her hands moved to her nipples and rolled them between her fingers. Her pussy ached. She slid two fingers into its sticky, swollen folds. It was time to get to work. But not here.

She rolled over and rose to her feet, completely unprepared for the sight that greeted her.

Watching her from not more than twenty feet away were two tanned and muscled men; probably the two figures Mandy had seen earlier and since forgotten all about in her carnal liaison with Neptune. She felt a blush rush up her neck, not only at the thought of what they must have seen, but because they were naked. Their big cocks curved over their balls in distinct arousal. Grinning, they turned away to continue their shoreline walk.

Mandy hurried back up the beach to her hideaway, hornier than ever. She towelled herself down, then quickly checked the beach in both directions. The men had almost disappeared from view, and there was no-one else in sight. She stretched out on the damp towel and basked in the sun's weakening rays. It had to be getting on for eight o'clock now, so sunset wasn't far away, a couple of hours, maybe. She suddenly realised how tired she was. It had been a long day.

She spread her legs and trailed her hands down over her belly to the place that demanded attention. Her breasts squeezed pleasingly between her upper arms, she slid the four fingers of her left hand into her hot, slippery cunt. With the index finger of her right hand, she went to work on the pink, shiny nub at the base of the sliver of pubic hair. Images of cocks filled her mind: the cocks of the men on the beach; Teddy's lovely cock, pre-cum trickling down the shiny purple glans; the tractor driver's gleaming torso and bulging jeans...

The tractor crawled by, the driver's stiff cock rearing up from his flies like a giant snake. "Oooh, mademoi*selle*! Très belle! Très, très *belle*!"

Mandy glanced down at her breasts, wondering what she was doing back in her car on that narrow road, sitting there completely naked...

"Très belle..."

The sound of the tractor engine faded into the sound of crashing surf. Mandy opened her eyes.

"Très, très belle."

It was the two naked men from the beach, standing one either side of her. She'd fallen asleep.

Before she could gather her wits, one of the men spoke. "Je suis Philippe." He pointed at his friend. "C'est Jean." He smiled a perfect white smile. "Vous êtes très belle."

Mandy stifled a laugh. Here she was, naked, and with fingers stuffed inside her sticky cunt, and a couple of Frenchmen were introducing themselves as if they came across this sort of thing every day!

"Je suis Mandee," she said, wondering briefly if she was either still dreaming, or losing her mind.

The pair looked down at her, their hungry eyes questioning. Mandy stared up at their big stiffening cocks, her nipples growing hard. Heart thumping, she spread her legs wider, a universal signal for 'I want cock and I want it now'.

Philippe and Jean knelt beside her. Philippe stroked her face and kissed her mouth with a sensuality that blew her away. If only British men could kiss like that! As his tongue twisted and probed, Jean used his to lick her heaving breasts. Mandy groaned as teeth gently nipped a nipple. Philippe covered her cheeks, her nose, her eyes in kisses then drew back, showing Mandy his huge, fully-erect cock. She grasped it with her left hand and began to pump.

Jean stopped sucking her nipples and shuffled up until his hard, veiny monster hung over Mandy's face. Still pumping Philippe's iron erection, Mandy reached for Jean's with her hungry mouth. Jean gasped and pushed himself in and out, in and out. Mandy's pulsing hole bubbled with fuck juice.

Breathing heavily, Philippe stayed Mandy's pumping hand. "Non, non…"

He crawled down between her legs and circled his

tongue along the inside of her thigh. Mandy tensed, desperate for Philippe to touch her, lick her, suck her. Then his mouth was clamped around her labia, his tongue flicking rapidly over her swollen clit and in and out of her gaping hole.

Then it was Jean's turn to stop her with a reluctant "Non!" and he pulled his cock from her mouth.

Mandy writhed and groaned beneath Philippe's expert manipulation of her oozing cunt. Oh, how she needed cock! If only she knew enough French to ask!

But they knew what they were doing.

Philippe looked up from between her legs, his mouth wet and shiny with her juices, and indicated that she should stand. Sign language. He must have realised from her awful accent that she wasn't French. Thank goodness. It would save a lot of hassle.

Trembling, Mandy stood, deliciously conscious of the juices trickling down her thighs and buttocks. Philippe lay down in her place, motioning her to sit on him. When she straddled him, facing him, he shook his head and pointed at his feet. Mandy turned around and lowered herself onto him, filling herself with hot, hard cock. She almost screamed with the sheer pleasure of it, and began to slide up and down on him, her fingers massaging her slippery swollen clitoris. But Philippe had other ideas. He pulled her down on top of him from behind, his hands caressing her tits. Jean knelt between her legs and indicated that she should lie flat, with her legs on top of Philippe's.

When she was in position, Philippe began to move his hips beneath her. Mandy quickly found the rhythm, and began to match him, stroke for stroke. Jean ducked his head between her thighs and thrust his tongue against her dripping clitoris. This time, she did cry out. It was exquisite: Philippe's rasping breath hot on the back of her neck... his hands massaging her tits... his huge cock thrusting in and out of her, faster and faster... Jean's warm mouth sucking… tongue lapping…

Philippe bucked beneath her and emptied his balls with a long groan. Mandy began to orgasm. Jean struggled to his knees and began to wank over the writhing pair, his other hand massaging Mandy's swollen clit. His eyes closed, his mouth opened, and creamy spunk shot from the end of his thick cock, over Mandy's tits, belly and cropped pubic hair. Gasping for breath, he collapsed onto the towel beside her and Philippe.

They lay there for several minutes, basking in a warm sexual afterglow and listening to the surf crashing on the beach.

Philippe kissed the back of Mandy's neck. "Très belle," he whispered.

Mandy eased herself off Philippe's cock with a happy sigh. British men would never dream of telling a girl she was beautiful after the event. Before, yes. But never after.

Her towel inaccessible beneath their spent bodies, Mandy decided to clean up in the sea. As she left the hollow, murmured conversation drifted to her ears.

"Jesus, Phil, these French girls really go."

"They sure do, John. I just wish I spoke the lingo properly, mate."

Mandy's mouth dropped open in surprise. Then she gave a rueful grin. Perhaps she wouldn't generalise quite so much about her countrymen in future!

Suddenly aware of the changing light, she stood on the shoreline and watched a fiery orange sun sink into a sea reflecting hues of gold and crimson back to the sky. The brochure was right: the sunsets really were spectacular.

Bamboobzled
by Landon Dixon

She stopped me in the hall, just as I was shoving the key into the lock.

"Jim Brubaker – PI?" she queried, in a phone sex kind of voice. Her body backed up the voice, and then some.

She was Brinn Stones, breast-blessed star of the silver screen, and every guy's wet dream from here to Eternity, Iowa. Her long, blonde tresses were neatly weaved into a ponytail, her voluptuous body poured into a red, latex dress that highlighted her queen-sized tits in blazing neon, her slim, black-stockinged legs cascading out of the thigh-high bottom of the devil-dress.

"I'm Brubaker," I admitted, stocking up on enough eye candy to permanently rot my rods and cones.

"I need your help," Brinn breathed, her green eyes flashing 'go'. She took a deep breath, and her deep breasts stirred the cream in my cockles.

I wiped drool off my dimple, pushed the door open.

We settled down in my inner-office, me behind my battered, metal desk, Brinn perched on the edge of a battered, wooden client chair, her slender, noir-shaded legs crossed like my fingers.

"What's the trouble?" I asked, and she told me, in explicit detail – after first swearing me to client confidentiality.

Apparently, little Miss Stones had gotten drunk at a recent house party and been badly taken advantage of. Someone had tossed her a hunk of fresh female and she'd leapt at the fishy bait, the someone lensing the resulting Lesbo-Sapphic wrestling match, unbeknownst to Brinn, for posterity and profit. Rumours of the taped tryst had not-so-subtly surfaced in the Tabs soon after, followed by a blackmailer-to-Brinn phone call demanding one million dollars for the safe return of the sex footage.

Brinn wanted me to track down the compromising tape, before it went public. Seems her career wasn't flying anywhere near as high as her lifestyle, and she couldn't cobble together a million bucks with a handgun and a Richard Nixon mask. And, oh yeah, the same two con artists – the muff diver and the shutterbugger – had also made off with Brinn's rather extensive sex toy collection.

"You'll find the tape and my toys, Mr Brubaker?" Brinn asked at the end of her spiel, her cherry-red lips parted breathlessly.

"Jim," I said. "You bet I will. Four hundred dollars a day plus expenses."

She batted her lashes like a silent film heroine tied to a railway track. "I'm, uh, afraid I can't afford that … Jim," she snuffled. "Perhaps we can arrange another, um, form of payment?"

I wasn't one to turn my snoot up at post-dated cheques, and was about to say so, when the impetuous babezilla stood up and unzipped her crimson second-skin, let it slide down and off her porn star body like she was unveiling a bust. And what a bust! Her tits were big and bronze and boldly upright, pressure-capped by jutting, mocha nipples that cried out for suction.

She cupped her huge, nude, sun-kissed boobs, rolled rigid nipples between slender, scarlet-tipped fingers like they were .44 calibre cartridges. My mouth cracked dry as the Hollywood Hills, my throat clicking like a camera when

I swallowed.

Brinn sensuously slid a pair of lacy, black panties down her long, luxurious, silk-clad legs, revealing a baby-faced pussy already glistening with anticipation. I admired everything about her as she strolled around my desk, up to me. She grabbed one of my sweaty paws and pulled me to my feet, then abruptly planted her glossy lips square-on my agape pucker.

"I like the way you pay your bills, baby," I mumbled, wrapping her burning body in my arms.

Her thunderous tits pressed hard and soft and hot into my manly chest, and we kissed like the war had just ended – and we'd won! Then Brinn darted her silver-tinted tongue in between my mouth flaps, and we frenched as they do on the Continent.

I broke her tongue-lock, brought my kisser down for an intimate talk with her titanic tits, grabbing hold of her breasts and happily squeezing and kneading them – almost passing out from disbelief when I found the fleshy pair as natural as organically-grown melons. They were firm and fun to play with, and after fondly manhandling them for a while, I stuck out my tongue and flicked it at one of the sex kitten's engorged nipples.

"Suck my tits!" Brinn hissed, excitedly rubbing my buzzcut, brewing up a static-electric storm.

I vacuumed her jutting right nipple into my mouth, sucked on it like a parched dairy farmer desperate to draw milk. Then I shifted over to her other nipple, repeated the succulent process, bobbed my bean back and forth between her bountiful boobs, sucking and tonguing sweet, swollen nipple like I'd never been taught how to use a glass.

"Fuck my tits!" Brinn shrieked.

I unhanded and unmouthed the gorgeous girl's saliva-soaked jugs and jutters and fumbled my pants open, and she quickly pulled my cock out of my shorts, started stroking.

"Yeah, baby!" I gritted, her hot little brown hand sliding

easily and expertly up and down my throbbing, pink dong.

She dipped to her knees, added some tongue to her handiwork, teasing the bloated tip of my dick with the playful tip of her tongue. She tickled my slit, the sensitive underside of my prong where shaft meets hood, before inhaling my mushroomed cap and tugging on it.

"Talk to me, baby!" I groaned, clutching her silky, yellow hair, urging her on.

She gobbled down more and more of my meat, till she had a good three-fourths of little big Jim lodged in her talented mouth and throat. Then she began moving her head back and forth in a rhythm as old as original sin, blowing me like she was Divine Brown and I Hugh Grant. Her puffy lips slid to and fro on my pulsating shaft, over and over, one of her hands gripping and probing my ass, the other juggling my balls.

I'm an impatient knob at the best of times, and I was soon all-too-ready to blow my top. So I yanked my dripping dong out of Brinn's mouth and growled, "How 'bout that tit-fuck?

She smiled up at me, hefted her massive mams, and I ploughed my greasy pole in between them. I covered her hands with my hands, shoved her heated hooters over top of my raging cock, started sliding my rock-hard member in and out of her awesome tit-tunnel.

"Fuck my tits!" she hollered again, spitting down at my dick, into her golden cleavage.

I churned my hips like a casting couch director, urgently tit-fucking the showstopper of a gal, and she stuck out her tongue, providing a warm, wet cushion for my peek-a-booing cocktop. Then I bleated like an agent come contract renewal and blasted white-hot jizz onto Brinn's heaving chest, into her open mouth, all over her magnificent mounds.

"You'll find the tape and my toys?" she asked rhetorically, milking my spent dick with her hand, licking a last pearl from my slit.

"Consider them found," I grunted, holstering my empty weapon.

I made some calls to the boys in the boing-boing business. The question was simple: anyone approach you about marketing a sex tape starring Brinn Stones? Brinn and I both knew that even if she actually paid off her illicit filmographer, he was still likely to stiff her by distributing a copy of the dirty tape. That's how blackmailers work, after all, why they top the charts along with politicians and paedophiles on most everyone's billboard of scumbags.

Initially, I got nothing more than confirmation that a buzz was definitely building about Brinn's alleged blue movie, but then I crossed wires with Hector Gonzalez, and got so much more. "How's the porn business, compadre – up and down?" I joked into the blower.

"This your one call from the joint?" Hector responded.

Gonzalez owned a string of adult video and sex toy stores in the rougher 'hoods. I told him what I was looking for, and he said, 'join the crowd'. "No one's tried to peddle you a homemade sex tape lately, huh?" I mused.

"I didn't say that, bro. I've bought four upskirt and three women's washroom spy cam flicks in the last two days alone," he boasted. Hector considered himself the Long John Silver of pirated porn. "But I haven't been offered any Brinn Stones epic, muchacho."

I frowned, fingered the next name on my list. "Okay, thanks anyway. Don't take any wooden buttplugs, eh."

"Yeah … hey, funny you mention that. Some guy was just trying to sell me a shitload of sex toys not half-an-hour ago. Can you believe it, bro – used sex toys!"

I bolted upright. "Know him?"

"Nope. But he's still here – at my store on Figueroa. The cashier just gave him enough quarters to choke a chicken – for the video booths in back."

I gunned it over to Hector's garbage bag-curtained jerk joint on Figueroa like a bat into hell. And after feeding my friend a pair of twenties, he finally pulled out a zebra-striped, double-headed dong that he'd only recently purchased for repackaging and resale. He pointed the dildo-built-for-two at the rear of his store, where the video booths were located. I hefted the psychedelic pussy-pleaser, mentally ticking it off the voluminous list of missing pleasure tools Brinn had given me. Then I ambled to the back of the store, down a dimly-lit, booth-flanked, grunting and groaning corridor where men were getting their jollies off, free Kleenex provided.

A quick peek over the tops of the booths, and I soon spotted the red, peeling, bald head I was looking for. I tossed the eighteen-inch twat-snake over the wall and it landed in Baldy's unzipped lap. He took one gander at the funky-coloured man-substitute and jumped up and shot out of the booth. I caught him by the collar, used his sunburned head to lever the emergency exit door open.

"Where'd you get the hardware, cueball?" I barked, slamming him against the cement wall of Hector's sex-market.

"I don't know nuthin'!" he squealed, squinting up at me, the glaring LA sun roasting his red-rimmed eyes. His stubby body was clothed in a phlegm-stained 'Free Tommy Chong' T-shirt and a pair of greasy, black jeans.

"Normally, I'd buy that," I said. "But the poon-pump you been peddlin' tells me you know where the Brinn Stones' sex tape is hiding. And I want it!"

He polluted the air with pleas of innocence for a short while longer, till a well-placed right with a cinder-block shoulder behind it sent him reeling into a row of garbage cans. From there, it took only a couple of size-twelves to the ribs to get him singing like an American Idol.

His name was Richard Waud, a sometime

cinematographer and full-time hustler. His last gig had seen him use his stolen digital camcorder to record a clit-to-clit tango between actress-wannabe Sheila Storm and actress-wanna-eat Brinn Stones. He claimed it was my client's idea – a sordid attempt to cash in on her fast-fading screen cachet, maybe even resuscitate her career somewhat, by creating a buzz about her bare-assed shenanigans and then selling the sex file for a hefty premium on the Internet. The way Waud spewed it, Brinn was desperate and destitute, and for a cut of the proceeds, he was hired to exercise his skills behind the camera and in front of the computer, play the role of Brinn's secret agent.

It was a dirty little yarn, complete with matching double-crosses – Waud's confessed plan to sell Brinn's toys and tape for his benefit alone, and Brinn's siccing a dick on Waud to get the tape back all for herself – and I mulled it over like bread dough as Waud and I walked the short distance to his dingy apartment. Once there, he unlocked a tickle trunk jam-packed with enough sex toys to render men obsolete, plucked out a camcorder cassette labelled 'BS'. He plugged it into his PC, and the screen lit up with the eye and zipper-popping 'Brinn Loves Sheila' story. The plot was thin, the dialogue scanty, but the character development was triple-X, double-D dimensional.

I confiscated the cassette and the toys, smashed the computer and the camcorder, leaving Waud to pick up the pieces of his shattered life.

I drove back to the office, pulled up a chair and bottle, and pondered the case developments. I soon decided the best course of action was some late-night surveillance, see if I couldn't locate the truth somewhere in the shadows.

So, come eleven p.m., I motored on over to Brinn Stones' palatial estate on Sunset. I crossed a broken glass welcome mat atop a perimeter security fence, then made like a F117, landing in some shrubbery alongside a boob-shaped swimming pool. And even before I could do a window check, I ogled the answers to a lot of my questions: my client and the equally chesty Sheila Storm dashing out of the mansion in their all-together and diving into the swimming pool.

My eyes strained along with my dick as I watched the buxom duo, who were obviously far from strangers, frolic about in the twinkling, lamp-lit water. The breasty girls met up in the centre of the pool, and Brinn grabbed Sheila in her arms and laid a tongue-lashing on the redhead's gaping mouth. Sheila returned her boob-buddy's wet-hot fire, the two babes swapping spit and swiping tongue like it was second nature. It looked very much like Waud had been puking the truth, unless Brinn had actually been too wasted to realise she and her playmate had been filmed.

Brinn splashed over to the side of the pool, hoisted herself up, and plopped down on the edge of the swim tank, her legs dangling in the water. She gestured at Sheila, and the flame-haired girl swum over, in between Brinn's smooth, sun-burnished legs, dove tongue-first into her lover's sodden pussy.

"Yes! Eat me, Sheila!" Brinn howled at the moon, wrapping her hands and legs around Sheila's head.

Sheila gripped the juggsy blonde's thighs and really went to town on her pussy, digging her tongue in deep, rubbing the belle of Hollywood Boulevard's clit with her thumb, reaching her other hand up to squeeze and tease Brinn's breasts, tweak and twirl her protruding nipples. Brinn moaned with pleasure, her hand grasping Sheila's hand on her splayed titties, pulling it up to her mouth to anxiously suck on the slender fingers, as Shelia earnestly licked her slit.

Brinn finally pushed Sheila back, and then helped her out of the pool, allowing me to eyefuck the finest heart-shaped ass I'd ever seen. The two slippery, top-heavy ladies bounded over to a giant air mattress. Brinn pushed Sheila down on top of it, then climbed aboard herself. Brinn positioned Sheila's pole dancer's legs, and her own lush body, such that her shaved snatch met Sheila's trimmed, ginger bush in a love embrace. The naughty film star then started pumping her hips, lustily grinding her pussy into Sheila's pussy.

"Fuck me, Brinn!" Sheila screamed, staring wildly up at her lover's sex-contorted face.

I eagerly surveyed Brinn's plump, undulating ass, her flexing cheeks, Sheila's busy hands gripping and groping Brinn's round chest-mounds. Hard-on cases like these were as rare as silicon-free San Fernando Valley movie sets, and I almost burst my zipper with pride at a job very well done when Brinn collapsed on top of Sheila, savagely kissed and frenched the ultra-endowed redhead, her hips still churning up a storm. The busty babes were glistening tit-to-tit, damp, pointed nipples rubbing against damp, pointed nipples, Brinn relentlessly pounding Sheila's poon with her poon, their tongues thrashing together.

"God almighty!" Brinn exploded, her body jerking violently as she pussy-frictioned herself to orgasm.

Sheila wasn't far behind, the voluptuous fuck-doll wailing with joy, digging her fingers into Brinn's trembling butt cheeks, her body jolted repeatedly by girl-inspired ecstasy. Both wicked women's mountainous jugs jounced around like they were electrically charged, till Brinn finally tumbled off of Sheila and onto her back, wasted.

I exited my peep position at that point and strolled up to the nude, lewd mattress-thumpers, tossed the zebra-striped dildo down onto Sheila's slick bumpers. "Anyone for round two?" I asked, smiling back at the shocked look on Brinn's face.

After sending her fuck-bunny home, and after some half-hearted denials, Brinn finally admitted her treachery. "Hype sells," she stated succinctly, like any Hollywood mogul with moss where morals once grew. She stood in the middle of her spacious, avant-garde-appointed living room, her built-for-sex body swaddled in a bathrobe. "The sex tape blackmail story, the leaks to the Tabloids – that was all about creating excitement, to maximise box office receipts."

I stared at the droll doll's unrepentant expression. Her face, sans make-up, looked washed-out and plain. I said, "So you produced the sex film willingly, with your girlfriend Sheila as co-star and your movie lot acquaintance Waud as cameraman? Knowing full well that you were going to stiff Dick out of his promised take of the gross by sending a big, mean PI after him, or feeding him to the wolves if something went wrong?"

"Richard would've double-crossed me," Brinn replied, shrugging her shoulders. "He stole my sex toys … and was already selling them, wasn't he? Show biz is a dog-eat-dog business, Jim. And I intend to make millions off this," she held up the cassette I'd given her, "so I can get out."

I believed that like I believed reality shows were real. "I could go to the cops, or the press," I muttered.

"You wouldn't break client confidentiality, would you, Jim? You hardboiled PIs live by a code, I thought? Not to mention the fact that your licensing board might not look favourably on you accepting sex in-lieu of payment." She deftly opened the robe, let it slide off her buff, bare shoulders, fluttered fingers across her swelling, brown nipples. "And speaking of which … I'm willing to give you a bonus for all your hard work, Jim – just so there's no hard feelings."

I gazed at Brinn's gargantuan, golden orbs, as Daedalus once gazed at the sun, and it wasn't my feelings that got hard. My own private dick compelled me to accept her offer.

Brinn Stones mentioned something about PIs living by a code, and she was right. And part of that code dictates that

134

you don't let your client screw you around, hire you under false pretences to do their dirty work. So, before Brinn could sell any shares in her girl-girl goldmine, I sent the copy I'd downloaded onto my laptop to every adult chatroom, bulletin board, and file-sharing site I could Google, thus devaluing her sexy product by about 99.9%. Call it payback, call it a public service to hard-working, hand-cranking horndogs everywhere. All I know is that Brinn still ended up getting a chunk of her career back from the resultant publicity, and I got all of my self-respect.

Pretty Young Things
by Cathryn Cooper

The crowd from London duly arrived and, once dinner was over, glasses clinked and the gramophone was belting out some pretty lively music. It was 1927 and they were young, vigorous and out for some fun.

Drink flowed and dancing feet and wandering hands became more energetic as the evening went on.

Carew was content to drink too much, dance too much, and let providence take its sexual course. But, as at all parties, there is always that point and always that person that suggests a different distraction.

It was a ginger-haired, fresh faced young man named 'Polo' Gibbons who suggested having a car race and Carew, badly in need of diversion, seconded his suggestion.

'Ten pounds bet!' exclaimed Polo as he slammed two gleaming white five-pound notes on the table.

'Seconded!' cried someone else, and did the same.

Other bets followed among a chorus of enthusiasm from male and female guests alike.

'You are a brave man indeed,' Carew said. 'Seeing as your forte is to have a horse between your legs and to be hitting a ball from one end of a field to another.'

There was immediate laughter when Polo commented that horses were not the only thing he had between his legs.

'Enough of your boasting, Polo,' Carew went on once

the laughter had died down. 'If you insist on racing then a-racing we will go. We will race out to the abbey ruins and have a midnight supper there. It will most definitely make a change. Things are getting a bit humdrum here.'

Saying that, he reached out and hit the needle arm from off the same old record. 'If I hear that bloody 'Black Bottom Rag' one more time, I shall kick that bloody gramophone all round the bloody room!'

Carew, who had already drunk more than his fair share, swigged back another large glass of brandy. He tottered a bit as he reached for his motoring things from the ever-present Imran, his faithful servant.

As he pulled on his gloves and slapped his goggles onto his head, he ordered the man to prepare a hamper and more drink and bring it out in the Bentley to the old ruins. He would take the Bugatti which was red and seated only two, but was faster than any car to be driven by his contemporaries.

The male guests dashed for their greatcoats and goggles, the women for their close-fitting hats and their silky summer coats.

Carew would usually have dallied over who he invited to share his car with him, taking glorious delight in the way each woman vied for his attention. As it was, tonight was different.

Surprisingly, it was Suzanne he invited. Suzanne was always there for the plucking – or suchlike. Normally, he would have gone for a girl he had not had sexually, but his brain was befuddled by too many glasses swigged down too quickly.

'Tallyho,' Carew shouted as he let go the handbrake and sped off down to the main gate.

Other engines roared into life behind and skits of dust wafted upwards to the lines of beech trees that bordered the road.

The moon hung low and the sky was bright. The road

was practically empty except for the brace of cars spewing from the gates of Thompson Towers, Carew's ancestral home.

The night would have been quiet except for the drivers and passengers singing, laughing and waving their arms, and being everything gay, young things were supposed to be.

Winding and steep, the road they travelled followed the line of the river. As they cornered and the tyres screamed, they dropped down that little bit more. Now and again, a roadside rabbit would run to safety, its eyes glinting like chips of amber in the glare of the headlights.

Surrounded on all sides by thickly forested hills, the road snaked to the valley floor.

Down in the valley, and near the river, the ruins of the abbey pointed darkly at the sky.

All the way, Suzanne had clung to Carew's arm. Her closeness unnerved him. With sober clarity, he recalled the day he had seen her being rogered by his head groom. But it wasn't so much what *she* had been doing that occupied his mind. Despite the amount of drink he had consumed, his cock hardened in his pants.

'This is wonderfully spooky, darling,' cooed the over attentive Suzanne as they pulled up before the crumbling stones. 'Do you think it's haunted, Carew darling?'

'No, you stupid bitch. The only spirits here tonight are the ones we've brought with us.'

With a dumb look on her painted face, Suzanne stared at him. 'You what?'

'Spirits,' he said, taking his flask from his coat pocket. He toasted her health and drank half its contents.

His head reeled, so he closed his eyes, then he threw back his head and opened them again. The skeleton of the abbey filled his eyes. Perhaps she was right, he thought. Perhaps it was haunted.

Gaunt and glassless windows of what had been the nave

framed a bright moon that seemed to hover above the blackness of the hills.

As other cars swerved to a halt on either side of them, he felt Suzanne's fingers run down over his shirt to the front of his trousers. He groaned, appreciative that her touch had momentarily dispersed his thoughts.

Suzanne groaned too. What she found there was far larger than she had expected.

'My!' she exclaimed, her eyes wide with delight. 'Now that is what I call a hard-on. I sure didn't know I had that good an effect on you!' At the same time as kissing his cheek, she tightened her grip.

'An offering,' Carew shouted. He escaped her grip and got out of the car. 'Let us go forth and make an offering on the altar to the old gods!'

He grabbed hold of Suzanne, then held the giggling girl at arm's length, his fingers tight around her wrist. Not that she seemed to mind very much. She was laughing more loudly now, her eyes bright with expectation as they darted from him, to the ruins and to the rest of their crowd.

'Look what I've got,' cried one dizzy redhead whose lipstick colour differed little from her hair. 'Fizzy,' she shouted. 'I've got fizzy.' She held a bottle of champagne at arm's length in each hand. A whoop of delight went up from the crowd. 'I thought you would all approve, darlings. In fact I knew you would!'

'She's drunk. She's bloody drunk,' cried Carew, and wondered why he found it so funny.

Laughing and giggling, the redhead led the merry throng among the fallen stones and through the Norman arch that had once had a door in it. Arched, glassless windows framed the dark sky outside.

In total darkness if would have been frightening. As it was, the moon shone but did little to ease the overall eeriness of the place.

Carew, dragging the giggling Suzanne, reached the

jagged stone that had once been the altar. Once there, he grabbed a bottle of champagne from the redhead and took a mighty swig.

'A libation,' he shouted, champagne trickling down his chin.

'What?' cried Suzanne, still laughing, still dancing around as the music was still playing.

'We'll do a play,' Carew shouted. 'We'll do something very old, very haunting, and we'll start with a sacrifice!'

Turning to Suzanne, he curled his fingers over the front of her very low-cut dress, pulling it down so that her nipples popped out in full view.

Suzanne played her part, feigning fear. 'Oh, sir. Take pity on a poor virgin, sir. Please!' As she pleaded, she nimbly slipped out of her dress.

'I will be a naked sacrifice,' she cried, her hair flying and all the dizziness of drink in her eyes and her actions.

Completely unabashed, she proceeded to take off her clothes until only her stockings and her garters remained.

A sheen of sweat covered her body which, touched by the light of the moon, made it shine like silver. Her breasts were pretty and of average size. Her belly curved gently down to her posy of pubic curls.

There was egging on from those gathered, saucy suggestions, and other comments that were downright lewd. Not that Suzanne seemed to mind. Exhibitionist to the end, she dropped naked to her knees before Carew. Clinging to his legs, she bent low, her bottom high. It shone before his eyes. Those who watched gasped with delight, and Suzanne giggled as couch grass and virulent weed tickled her breasts. Carew smiled disdainfully as she kissed his shoes, his knees and the hidden lump behind his flies.

'Bitch!'

One word brought the laughter to a mere trickle as the man who had accompanied Suzanne to the party lay the flat of his hand across her rump.

Suzanne yelped.

Silence descended on those watching. Anticipation replaced ribald laughter. Everyone was responding to the moment, holding their breath, waiting excitedly to see what would happen next.

Her escort, a man named William, slapped her behind again. 'Go on, you slut. Get on with it. There's a queue forming to get into you and seeing as I lost the bet to be first here, I'm first to put my own engine into you.'

William proceeded to undo his trouser buttons.

Carew stepped back into the shadows, as fascinated as anyone to see what would happen next.

For some reason, he no longer wished to be part of the crowd. He wanted to watch this as though he were alone, a voyeur paying for the privilege.

No one noticed him drifting into the shadows. From there he watched unseen as the man lay Suzanne out on the stone altar.

Chloe, Mary and another girl whose name Carew did not know, plus one of the men, were holding Suzanne's hands and feet as William stabbed into his sacrifice with his very own weapon. Too much wine and too much excitement; he jolted his delivery and, when he had finished Suzanne's body was white and exposed, her nipples staring at the stars, her crisp covering of pubic hair stirred by the breeze.

She did not remain exposed for long. Another man took William's place. With obvious appreciation, Suzanne arched her back as his penis thrust between her open thighs.

The first man who had pushed himself into Suzanne was now recovered and ejaculating over her rather than in her. A third man was waiting to take his place.

With a sense of having seen it all before, Carew retired completely from the throng, finding coolness and calm by melting further into the shadows.

Eventually he was alone. Even the moon did not pick him out from the blackness. He liked this. It was spellbinding, almost magical.

He felt his way along the stones, imagining other times, other people who had been here. He looked towards the moonlight, not noticing anything around him. The spell was suddenly broken. Fingers – cool, feminine fingers flat against the wall.

'Who's that?' he asked, sure it must be one of the others.

He strained his ears and heard breathing.

'I know someone's there,' he said, determined not to be panicked. 'Stop playing around. I know it's you.'

The fingers touched his again. This time he grabbed them and pulled the other person towards him.

'Tell me who you are,' he said.

'No.'

Her voice was soft. Her breath sweet.

He held her waist tightly, unwilling to give her the chance to escape.

'You're not wearing any clothes,' he said.

She did not answer, not in words. Her hips pressed against his. She took hold of his hand and placed it upon her breast. Her flesh was cool, the nipple hard as a rock. His cock stiffened in response.

Who was this?

Clinging firmly to his shoulders, she rocked her body forward to meet his, inviting him to take her. He needed no other invitation. Fingers all thumbs, he tore at his flies and got out his cock.

'For you,' he said, raised her slightly from the ground and pushed it into her.

The crispness of his pubes meshed and crackled with hers. Again and again his pelvis tapped and teased her hidden nub.

She grabbed hold of his hair, and pushed his mouth to her breasts.

A sudden thought occurred to him. 'You're not a ghost are you?'

143

He did not want and did not get an answer. He wanted to hold onto this moment. Whoever this was he would aim to hold onto her for future reference. This one single night would not be enough. He would want her again.

'You're incredible,' he breathed, his hand flat across her back, holding her close to him.

The softness of her body and rapidity of her breathing told him she was there, that she was real.

At least I have not pushed my penis into a dry joint in the abbey wall.

He tried to hold himself in check, to prolong the moment, to wait, to let it droop and then harden all over again. He tried to draw back, but she held him close.

'My lord,' she whispered. 'My lord. Spare me. No more. No more please.'

Her words took him by surprise. Her hips were still thrusting. 'You don't mean that do you?' He shook his head. Her body was still warm and inviting. Of course she didn't mean it.

'Have to say, the words work for me. Say them again. Go on. Plead with me to let you go free.'

'Please, my lord!' Her voice was a thin wail. My, but she really knew how to turn a guy on. What an actress. Far superior to Suzanne.

The pulse of life itself began rising up his stem, heating up, climbing like the liquid in a hot – a very hot – thermometer.

'I'm coming,' he shouted, throwing his head back and closing his eyes. 'I'm coming.'

He clung tightly to her, pressing his body against hers.

At last it was over. He was drenched in sweat, but hell, who cared, it was worth it.

Being a fairly considerate man, a sudden thought came to him. 'What about you? Did you come?'

She didn't answer.

He stepped back to pee and apologised for having to do

so.

'Look,' he said, reaching out for her once he'd finished. 'Do you think…'

His fingers touched only crumbling stone. 'Hey. Where are you?'

He looked around him. There was no way she could have gone without him knowing.

'Hey,' he shouted again.

The moon had shifted position. Its silvery light now fell on the wall where his phantom woman had been. In its light he saw a set of manacles hanging from the wall, the last vestige of hair clinging to a stone before the wind caught it and it blew away.

Wreck-Her
by Lynn Lake

If you've ever driven through southwestern Manitoba in the middle of summer, you know how hot and dry it gets – a desert-like inferno that forces gophers to doff their fur coats and seek shelter in shaded burrows. And it was all that and ten degrees more one cloudless July afternoon, halfway between Minnedosa and Brandon, when the rear axle on my company-leased SUV decided to snap in half.

I was on my way to wine and dine a client in Brandon, to try to convince him to carry some of our new lines, but when I stepped out of that broken-down vehicle, into that harsh, blazing cauldron of prairie heat, my thoughts shifted rapidly from schmoozing to survival. The temperature was a few degrees hotter than Hell, with nary a car on the shimmering horizons.

My cellphone only works in major cities, under perfect atmospheric conditions, so it was totally useless, of course. I anxiously scanned all four points of the compass, finally spotted what appeared to be a farmhouse a long way off in the distance, in the middle of one of the endless fields of sun-bleached wheat that lined both sides of the sizzling roadway. I started walking.

A hundred yards out, my business-casual blouse, skirt, and stockings were soaked with sweat and my high heels were off my feet and in my hands. Two hundred yards out, my butt was parked on the edge of the melting asphalt and I was rubbing my sore feet and thinking what a nicely-browned piece of roadkill I was going to make for some hungry coyote.

But five minutes of basting later, I was overjoyed to see an actual vehicle coming towards me from the south. I ran out into the middle of the road and frantically waved my arms, like anyone would've had a tough time making out a big-breasted blonde wind-milling her limbs under that glaring sun. The vehicle stopped for me, and miracle of miracles, it turned out to be a tow truck.

An oily-looking squirt with a sawed-off cigar stuck in a corner of his mouth climbed down out of the cab. "Somethin' wrong, ma'am?" he asked, ambling up to me. The overalls he wore were only slightly less greasy than his hair, and they, or him, were named Stan, according to the stitched-on tag.

"Yes! My SUV's broken down!" I panted. "Can you give me a tow into Brandon?"

Stan studied the grounded SUV through a pair of red-rimmed slits, then ogled my chassis up and down for awhile. Then he stared meaningfully into my green eyes, unplugged the midget cigar from his mouth, and stated, "Looks like a job I can handle, all right." He grabbed my hand and pulled me off the pavement and into the neighbouring wheat field.

It was obvious what the horny little grease monkey had in mind. And, to be frank, I was more than willing to accommodate him, if it meant a ride into a nice, cool beverage room in Brandon. So, when we'd tramped about thirty yards out into the waist-high waves of grain, and Stan had battened down a comfortable crop circle with his rather large feet, I slowly stripped off my blouse and bra, skirt, stockings, and panties. I stood before him proudly flaunting a body even riper than the surrounding wheat.

He stared hard at my heavy breasts, my jutting, pink

nipples, my downy, blonde pussy. "Cripes almighty! You're built like a brick shithouse, lady!" he complimented, before unzipping his overalls and revealing his own wiry form.

I cupped my low-slung tits and eyed the half-pint's rapidly inflating cock, watching in awe as it grew and grew and grew. This roll in the wheat was going to be a lot more fun than I'd originally thought. "You're a small man capable of big surprises, mister!" I enthused back at him. His erection topped out at the nine-inch mark, long and hard and pointing arrow-straight and accusing at my dampened slit.

Stan stumbled over the stubble and grabbed me in his short arms, kissed me hungrily on the lips. I gripped his head and crushed my mouth against his, the hot sun beating down hard on our blistering southern exposure. And after kissing, entwining our tongues together for a good, long, heated while, Stan pushed me down onto the bed of grain and climbed aboard, his face barely coming up to my chest.

"Mmmm!" I moaned, as he gripped my swollen breasts, tongued my engorged nipples.

He groped my tits and licked and sucked on my nubs, biting into and pulling on them, his huge cock pressing insistently into my stomach. I ran my hands up and down his rugged body, clawing at his back as he fed on my breasts. I latched onto his rounded butt cheeks, kneaded them.

"Fuck me," I breathed. I was as lubricated now as the warm, rich earth after a summer rainstorm. We were both bathed in sweat, the scratchy grain stalks sticking to our heated bodies.

Stan spat one of my ripened nipples out of his mouth and fumbled for his cock. I anxiously spread my legs in anticipation. He gripped his tremendous prick, jammed its mushroomed hood into my slit, shoving forward until he was entirely buried inside my pussy.

"Fuckin' A!" he growled, grabbing my saliva-slick boobs and churning his hips.

"That's the way!" I exclaimed, revelling in the wicked, over-full feel of his pistoning cock. I burned with a feverish, sensual heat more than sunshine-related.

Stan vigorously pumped me, his dirty hands groping my shuddering tits, his thick tongue lashing my obscenely swollen nipples, sweat pouring off his brow and splashing down onto my heaving chest. And just when my head started swimming and my body shaking with impending orgasm, he suddenly halted his wonderful work and asked, "You ever take it up the ass before, ma'am?"

It had actually been quite a long dry spell between anal sexings for me. So I pushed the little big guy off of me and scrambled up onto all fours. I reached back and clawed my big, plush bum cheeks apart, hissed, "Fuck me up the ass, Stan!"

He nodded eagerly. Then he spat in his hand a couple of times and polished his already slick prick. He pointed his cock at my puckered bull's-eye and steered it on target, pushing hard against my bumhole, until he had punched inside. I moaned, my legs trembling uncontrollably. I recklessly pushed back as he pushed forward, and his cock sank all the way into my tight chute.

A shiver of joy arced through me, his huge cock filling my ass like nothing that had ever come before. I planted my face in the fertile ground and frantically rubbed my clit, well-knowing that the languid feeling that now consumed my ass-violated body would soon be burnt off by scorching orgasm.

Stan moved his hips, sliding his monster cock back and forth in my anus, slowly at first, then faster and faster and faster. He held tight to my waist and pounded my bottom, the loud crack of his sweaty flesh against my rippling flesh sending crows wheeling and cawing into the blast-furnace air. He brutally plundered my ass, furiously sawing in and out of my chute. I desperately polished my tingling cum-button, a towering orgasm building within me.

"Yes! Yes!" I screamed, jolted by orgasm.

"I'm comin', too!" Stan cried, digging his nails into my flesh.

He fucked me in a frenzy, then exploded inside me, blasting white-hot cum deep into my trembling derrière. He came hard and long, like I did, filling me with his spunk.

When we eventually peeled ourselves apart again, brushed the seed and stalks and soil from our bodies and reclothed ourselves, Stan told me, "I'll have to use the radio to call a garage in Brandon, get them to send out a wrecker. See, the tow assembly on my rig's been busted for over a week now."

Mixed Blessings
by Phoebe Grafton

Horace always marked his calendar when we made love. This practice found its roots in his youth. Then, he was warned by his father, that too much sex could shorten his life span.

I estimate that at his present rate of progress Horace should outlive three monarchs, eight prime ministers and two appearances of Haley's Comet.

Horace developed mastery in terms of self control. He took a great deal of pride in the only body he, or anybody else, wanted to possess.

At such rare times when the calendar reminded and the moon was in the right quarter, Horace would prepare himself for the chosen day, normally a Saturday.

It was always before the morning news at eight o'clock. The countdown began. Horace would leave the bedroom whistling tunelessly. This was my signal to smile becomingly, brace myself or whatever.

Then he would return. He'd remove his bed socks, fold twice. Then arrange them neatly on the chair. This was followed by his pyjama trousers, folded along the crease, of course. Jacket next. Once he had established a neat pile, he would climb into bed – then on.

He would offer a few grunts, which I was expected courteously to join in.

1

A short crescendo, then – heigh ho, it was all over.

My reward – a quick hug followed by a peck on the cheek. I suspect he wanted to check that I was still breathing.

Horace would climb out of bed, clear his throat and mutter, 'That was splendid, my dear.' Then off to the bathroom he would march, all limp and tissued.

For my spouse then it was another milestone, another red biro mark on his calendar of life. It was all right for him. While the waves were crashing on his shore, my tide was still out.

There must be more to life than this, I thought. Yet the answer never came readily to me. The change in my fortunes was as sudden as it was inevitable

It was one of those dismal days in September. The battery in the alarm clock had expired. I was late for work on the very day that Horace decided it was time to trim his nose hairs.

I arrived in the office in a foul mood just in time for my computer to crash. Yvonne came to my rescue with a chocolate Brazil. Bless her.

Yvonne and I go back years. Not that we'd discussed our private lives much.

2

We did meet occasionally, however and took along our respective spouses.

With morale being low and bio-therms on the ebb, this was the day we were destined to give ourselves an ear bashing over lunch.

'I fancy doing a Shirley Valentine,' I said.

'Great,' Yvonne agreed. 'I get the holiday, you get the

Greek.'

'As if,' I scoffed, 'Don't tell me you'd turn down the prospect of a couple of days with a hunky Greek God?'

'Forget it,' she said, offering another chocolate Brazil.

'Off it are we?' I enquired politely.

'Off it? Off it, chance would be a fine thing. The man's insatiable.'

'Honestly?'

'Believe it.'

'What's insatiable anyway?'

'Y'mean Horace is no raging bull in the bedroom?'

'He's not even a raging tom cat. Remember that wild life programme on television where lions mate every half-hour for eighteen months?'

'Oh yes. Had to turn over. Trevor was watching.'

'Well there's not much lion in Horace. His idea is half an hour every eighteen months.'

3

'You're joking?'

'Oh, he's alright – but what wouldn't I give for a bit of passion.'

'You can borrow Trevor for a weekend if you like?'

We both stopped talking at that moment. It was as if both our minds locked into the possibility. I savoured the prospect for an instant. Trevor was a bit tasty after all. Wistful sighs arrived simultaneously.

'Ah, the peace,' breathed Yvonne.

'Ooh, the passion,' said I.

The silence was unbearable. I broke it.

'No, no we couldn't. We must be mad to even think about it.'

'Perhaps you're right,' Yvonne sighed.

She didn't offer any more chocolate Brazils after that. Misery lasted another twenty-four hours. I didn't get the chance to get my coat off in the morning when Yvonne dragged me off to the loo.

'Sod it,' she said with the sort of venom which ill matched her character. 'We'll do it – you can have Trevor for the weekend. He always fancied you anyway.' Her words were spoken with relish.

4

The fact that Trevor fancied me wasn't a bad start. Her enthusiasm was contagious.

'Look, I've been thinking. We are the same height, same sort of figure, and about the same dress size.'

So we went into detail. On the Friday we'd do a show together, have a meal and arrange to get home, or should I say each others homes, after the men folk had gone to bed.

To be on the safe side, in case of nosey neighbours, we'd change dresses. Finally we arranged to meet in the supermarket car park on Sunday morning and exchange front door keys.

Once we'd got down to the planning, it didn't seem half so frightening a prospect. Horace liked Yvonne. An attractive woman – pleasing to look at, was how he described her.

Thursday evening I caught Horace checking his calendar. My stomach turned somersaults. Such panic was short-lived. He was only confirming a dental appointment.

Friday at last! I dressed carefully. Horace noticed.

'You look splendid, my dear,' he observed.

'Yvonne and I are going out this evening.'

5

'So you are; I'd quite forgotten. Going straight from the office, are you?'

'Yes. We thought it would be easier. We are going for a

meal after the show. We might be a bit late. Will you be up?'

Did he notice my sharp intake of breath as I waited, inwardly quivering, for his answer? Apparently not.

'Shouldn't think so. Enjoy yourself. Tell me all about it over breakfast.'

The show was great, but who watched it? Certainly not Yvonne and I. We changed dresses in the loo at the theatre. I was not best pleased to note that she looked better in mine than I did.

It was a brief moment of discontent. After all she was getting Horace while I was getting greedy, hungry, lusty Trevor. It was a fair swap.

The witching hour finally came and the trap was sprung. We finished our small talk on the pavement outside the restaurant. Suddenly there was no more to say. We wished each other good luck, a brief hug for comfort – then Yvonne was gone.

As I put Yvonne's front door key in the lock I gave myself a thankful moment. At least the layout of the house was familiar to me.

6

The place was in darkness. Trevor was in bed.

A small moment of panic. Should I turn and run while there was still time? Then I thought of Horace and his calendar. Yvonne had got it right. Sod it!

In the bedroom there was little sound except Trevor's quiet breathing. I tiptoe around to my side, well Yvonne's actually – then quietly undressed.

Gingerly I felt around under the pillow for the nightdress. There wasn't one. Almost as gingerly I eased my naked body into the bed beside the sleeping Trevor. This is it, girl, I told myself apprehensively, but such thoughts were fleeting.

The man had built in radar. Hardly had I settled myself when Trevor turned over sleepily and reached out for me. His hand rested lightly at first.

As the sleep left him, the hand began to trace soft patterns across my skin. First up, then down. I liked that. I moved to his touch, a growing need swiftly replacing anxiety.

The searching fingers moved upwards once more and found my nipples. His hand smoothed over the contours of each breast in turn. Then his attentions focused on each nipple.

Pinching each, Trevor brought a firm response. So this was foreplay?

Below, I could feel a stirring, sensual need.

7

This unusual feeling of desire increased as he moved his head. He took each nipple in turn, placing moist lips over each and drawing to bring further response.

His hands sped downwards. The curled fingers sought, then found. Shock waves of pleasure coursed through me as he slipped his probing messenger into the moistness of my vagina.

By now I could both sense as well as smell the maleness of him. That sweet, evocative odour which only sensed to heighten my own desire. Such heady sensuality gave impetus to fresh boldness.

I reached across to follow the hair line across his belly. Yvonne forgot to tell me about this. Trevor was big. Not that I am an authority, you understand.

Running my hand up and down its length I marvelled in the darkness as the shaft bucked and twitched impatiently in my gentle grasp.

I wanted to play with the fascinating beast, tease it a little. Trevor's expert ministrations, however, gave hunger and my own impatience greater priority.

Trevor sensed as much. He uttered no more than a sigh. His lips sought to find my own in the gloom. My thighs parted a welcome.

8

He rubbed the pulsing head of his demanding organ across the lips of that part of my body which sought greedily to devour its tormenter.

Trevor remained poised above me for an instant, but it was an instant too long. I curled my legs about him, grasped high buttocks tightly and pulled him inside me.

I felt the head of his shaft slip beyond the lips. Together we moved and I was hugely, wonderfully full of him.

Control was out of the question as I matched his thrusting pace in the race for early completion. It seemed he was hardly inside me when our nearness became apparent.

No time to adjust to a sensual rhythm before I felt the vibrations deep within my own body, a body hungry to devour his all. Biting my lip I attempted to quell my rising excitement.

With a cry, a mixture of torment and exhilaration, I felt that glorious release. My contractions pumped the very soul of my lover, draining him to the last drop.

We spoke not a word as we lay side by side. For my part, I felt that words would shatter the magic of that very special moment. Sleep began to overtake me.

9

Just before it did, lying in the close comfort of the man beside me, I did offer up one silent, grateful thought. Thanks, Yvonne.

I awoke with the sunlight streaming through the curtains. At the same time as I was struggling with consciousness, my mind was trying to cope with the unfamiliar surroundings. When at last I grasped the situation I turned to see Trevor, propped up on one elbow, smiling down at me.

'Look,' I said. 'I know you think this is unusual.'

He didn't, least if he did he forgot to mention it. For at that moment of awakening, Trevor began once more to play wicked games with my responsive body.

Our foreplay assumed a mutuality which normally takes years to perfect. Here I was, after years in a wilderness of sexual indifference responding to Trevor as if we'd known both our sensitive areas through a relationship of long standing.

He had the sort of touch which sent shivers of anticipation right through me. We held, touched, caressed with such wise hands that our coupling became almost instantaneous.

I needed to feel his charging monster thrust deep inside me once again.

10

I wanted the fullness of his impatient loins grinding upon my own in ecstatic gyrations.

My hungry void once more devoured the man inside me. Our mutual release was a celebration, a promise of fulfilment to reward all my lost years.

All that sex made me ravenous. I tucked into a full breakfast. I thought of Yvonne. I had no doubt that Horace and Yvonne were sitting down to a very civilised breakfast.

She would try to look interested while he banged on about the economic situation in Albania. I looked across at Trevor. It was a warm moment. I knew where I'd rather be.

In my own home I could soak in a bath for hours. With Trevor it was a different ball game altogether.

Who needed hands when you had someone this

attentive? He washed my back, front, top and bottom. To show willing, I washed Trevor. The response was instantaneous. The man came complete with his own built in towel rail.

In the evening we went for a meal. Here the difference between Horace and Trevor became even more apparent. Horace always ate the same way as he lived, with meticulous detail.

I gazed around the crowded restaurant.

11

Crowded it might be, but this did not prevent Trevor playing those same wicked games beneath the tablecloth.

He traced exciting patterns on my inner thigh as we waited for each course to arrive. Throughout the meal he talked incessantly and ate one-handed. By the time dessert arrived, I could have bitten clean through the spoon.

Sex in the restaurant car park was almost a forgone conclusion. It wasn't easy. It was just as well we took the car. Even then it was difficult, but delightful.

The couple in the car parked next to ours obviously thought so as well. They didn't bother to go for a meal until we'd finished. I'd have preferred it if Trevor had left the interior lights off though.

By bedtime, on our return from the restaurant, I was beginning to think that the weekend had been well worthwhile. Tomorrow I would have to face the consequences when I returned home, but tomorrow was another day.

My sexual famine had been well and truly catered for. Excitement, passion and even novelty had given me the sexual fillip I so badly needed.

I knew that I should laugh about the car park experience for years to come.

12

Time to settle down for a warm, contented sleep to finish my perfect day.

Not quite, though. Once in bed I realised that Trevor's day had not yet drawn to a satisfactory conclusion. There was just one thing outstanding, and I could feel that pressing against me in the darkness.

My own well of passion had run dry. Yet since Trevor had afforded me so much pleasure over the weekend, it was the least I could do.

If I slept, it couldn't have been for long. Sometime in the middle of the night Trevor woke me again. If my grunts and sighs were somewhat off key, it was because I wasn't fully awake.

When dawn broke, Trevor once again chased my sleepiness away. I was beginning to feel like a rung-out dish cloth. All too quickly I began to feel sympathy for Yvonne's problems. Suddenly my fruitful weekend had turned into a nightmare.

The man was indeed insatiable. If he were mine on a regular basis I'd force feed him a bromide diet.

Escape was the only instant solution, so I fled to the bathroom. This time I didn't emerge until I washed, dressed and secured from toes to earrings.

After breakfast, I phoned Yvonne to confirm arrangements. She answered the phone.

13

'I can't talk right now,' she said. I assumed that Horace was in the close proximity.

I reminded her of the meeting time and place for our later meeting.

'Right.' Was all she said as if the words had been forced between clenched teeth. In any event, her voice sounded very distant. Then the phone went dead.

I left Trevor to do the breakfast dishes. He followed me out into the hall.

He put his arms around me. 'It's been a lovely weekend.' He said.

'Yes,' I agreed. It's been different.'

'What time do you have to meet Yvonne?' he asked with that look in his eye. Clearly Trevor was in the mood for a quick one for the road.

'Soon' I said.' Look I must go.'

We kissed. 'We ought to do this again,' he said, pressing against me.

'What a good idea,' I lied, pushing him away and opening the door.

'I'll miss you.'

'Me too.' I said with a straight face. 'Bye'

I parked at the agreed place. Yvonne drove up and stopped.

14

We exchanged keys and she drove off without uttering a word.

It occurred to me that Yvonne didn't look very rested for her few days of undemanding tranquillity with Horace. Perhaps her nerves had got the better of her.

What a relief it was to be home. Horace, I could hear moving about in the bathroom. I hoped he wouldn't be long. I wanted nothing more than a nice long peaceful – undisturbed soak in the bath.

In the bedroom I undressed slowly. I noted with pleasure all the familiar things I had taken for granted a few days earlier.

Horace's clothes were in a jumbled heap on the floor. Most unusual. As I was folding his clothes the way he liked them I noticed his torn calendar in the waste bin. Perhaps he'd torn it up in a fit of pique when he discovered me missing over the weekend. I had no time to give the matter further thought. The bathroom door opened.

Horace came into the bedroom wearing just a bathrobe. Also I noticed that he hadn't shaved for a day or two. Odd!

Before I had a chance to say hello, he'd discarded the dressing gown, throwing it carelessly into one corner.

15

He advanced, pushed me down upon the bed, swiftly divesting me of both knickers and bra.

This with an unfamiliar speed and purpose I'd not associated with Horace in the past.

Just as he began to devour my exhausted nipples, just as he attempted to bring my care worn body back to life, a fleeting thought permeated my reasoning.

First thing in the morning, I thought, when the shops are open, I'll rush out and buy Horace another calendar.

Blindspot
by Elspeth Potter

Being blind makes an orgy the most shattering experience in the world. In daily life, I'm always listening to the tap, tap, tap of my cane, listening for echoes, listening for movement, listening to hear if a truck is about to smash me flat. I'm always thinking: how to find the fridge, how to find the toilet, how to get to the bank. In the middle of an orgy, you can forget all that. You don't have to worry who's looking at you, seeing things about you that you can't see about them; everybody is looking at each other, for one purpose only, and the brush of unknown eyes becomes exciting. There's nothing to trip you up but pillows and bodies, no sharp edges anywhere for you to bump into; you can revel in the caress of different textures. It's a velvet universe of sighs and groans and sucking noises, and everywhere the miasma of bodily pleasure.

Everyone knows me at the swingers' club. Even though Sol and I divorced three years ago, women are always in demand and I continued to come here where everyone is in the dark. It's always warm in these rooms, and sound is muffled. It's a little like I imagine it must be in the womb, except for the smells. Mary Dubuque still wears the same fruity edible body paint she's stuck to for the last five years, and there's latex, and come, and lubricant, and mingling perfumes, and contraceptive foam, and the sharp stink of sweat.

Everybody knows to tell me their name when they approach, so I won't have to guess. There's a lot of uncertainty in not being able to see people, see their reactions and body language, so it's easier when they come to me, and I know I'm welcome. I need to be as welcome as possible.

I love the press of hot bodies to mine, the more the better. I like to get fucked from the back while someone else – a man, a woman, I can't see them, I don't care – sucks my tits, or even just lies beneath me like a live rug, feeling the impact each time hips slam into my ass. One day I'm going to try having two guys fuck me at once, one in my pussy and one in my ass, but not yet; maybe if someone else did it first, near me, so I could hear if she liked it.

Tonight was a little different than usual. Dante Baker had been to a store in New York City, and brought back a few toys. He told me about it, pressed up against my front while Marcus Viallo dry-humped my hip. Dante pressed something tiny into my hand. "It's a plug," he said. "Want to try it?"

Marcus, as usual, had a gigantic hard-on, and I could feel his heat through latex as he lazily stroked it over my buttock and pressed it into my hipbone. Dante had just fucked someone else, and I could smell it on him. They were distracting. "What else did you get?" I asked Dante, not able to think too hard about whether I wanted to try something new.

Dante curved his hands over my breasts and squeezed them lightly. I could tell from his voice that he was looking down at them. "I got a dildo," he said. "It's made out of silicon. I thought I might try it. In my ass. If you wanted."

Marcus started sliding his cock along the crack of my ass. I knew he was listening. Did that excite him? Did he want to fuck another man in the ass with a dildo? The thought had never occurred to me; I thought of dildos as something for women, had toyed with the thought of getting one but in the end sticking with my vibrator.

I thought about fucking Dante with a dildo, being the one doing to someone else for once, and my pussy creamed. Could I do that? Could I do it without screwing up and doing some stupid blind thing?

I tried to remind myself I was safe here, but it wasn't as easy as usual. I came here and did what I did, but I usually didn't do anything different. People knew what I liked.

Maybe I would like this. Maybe I would like it a lot. But I didn't want to screw it up. "Marcus," I said. "Marcus, will you help us?"

His cock slid to a halt in the small of my back. He leaned into me, sweaty chest and coarse hair against my shoulder blades, his mouth against my ear. "Oh, Becca," he said. "Can I fuck you first?"

I really wanted that huge cock splitting open my pussy lips and driving deep inside me, stretching me to the edge of my endurance, but if I did that now, afterward I would want to sleep, and Dante would find someone else. "After," I said, my heart speeding up. I hardly ever turned anyone down.

"Damn, you're killing me," Marcus said. "Okay, Dante?"

I could feel Dante's cock against my belly, giving little jerks and twitches. It seemed very much okay with him.

Dante stretched out on a pile of pillows and I stroked his spine, letting my hand stop on the rise of his ass. I decided straddling his legs would work better, so I did that, and held out my left hand for the dildo. Marcus gave it to me, covered with a condom and slippery with lubricant. I held out my other hand and he fitted on a latex glove, turned my hand over, and poured lubricant into the palm. Some of it dripped on Dante's back as I closed my hand to spread the lubricant all over my fingers, and Dante made a little noise. I liked that noise. I wanted him to make a lot more noise, so

I would know exactly what I was doing to him.

"Keep the lube ready," I said to Marcus, who was sitting beside me. I could feel his hot cock against my thigh.

He ran his hand down my back. It was slick, and I shivered a little as the air hit the wetness. Marcus didn't say anything, just patted my ass and took his hand away. "Dante, don't move," I said.

"Fuck," he said, his voice muffled by pillows. "Fuck, this is hot."

"She hasn't even done anything yet," Marcus said. His voice sounded strained.

"Just wait until it's you," Dante said.

I wanted to massage Dante's ass cheeks, but I had the dildo in one hand and a lubed glove on the other. I should have thought of that before. I would do it next time. I definitely wanted there to be a next time.

"Hold this for now," I said to Marcus, giving him the dildo.

I knew Dante's ass was right below me, just in front. I lowered my ungloved hand and very lightly traced until I found the crack and pulled my finger down it, forcing his cheeks apart. I rubbed the exposed skin with my gloved hand, leaving a wet trail behind. Dante's legs heaved a little and I clenched them with my thighs. I could probably find his hole by pressing in with my finger until something gave – and there it was. My pulse was thumping in my ears as I pressed a little harder and felt the rim of his hole grip my fingertip like tiny lips. It felt strange but very, very intimate; suddenly the tip of my finger was the most important part of me.

Dante gasped. "Stop?" I asked.

"No!"

I felt Marcus' hands in my hair, pulling it out of my face and letting it fall.

It took a while for me to get my finger in all the way. I imagined it was a cock fucking a tight pussy and pushed it

168

in smoothly and pulled out a little bit, not all the way so he wouldn't close up, pushing in a little more each time, listening to Dante's breathing get faster and deeper, and feeling Marcus' hot breath and skin: he was leaning over my shoulder, so close his hair tangled with mine. Every once in a while, he would slide his hand past my belly and squirt some more lubricant onto Dante's ass.

Each time I got in as far as I could reach, Dante would clench up and I'd be stuck for a moment, but if I waited, his muscle would relax and I could slide in a little more and he would make a whimpering sound that stabbed in my belly. The next time I could push in a little more.

After I added another finger, I had to stop for a minute and catch my breath. I was creaming all over Dante's legs; I could smell my own fragrance rising off his skin and mine.

I moved my two fingers faster than before, twisting them a little each time, then scissoring them open, making Dante stretch. He was grunting with each thrust now, just at the edge of my hearing. I added a third finger and worked him as hard as I dared, wondering if I could make him come just from this. I moaned myself at the thought.

It took me a moment to realise Marcus was speaking to me. "You can put in the dildo now. He wants it bad."

I wasn't sure I wanted his advice, but I wouldn't refuse it. In fact, I liked that Marcus was into this. "Dante, do you want me to use the dildo now? Do you want me to fuck you with the dildo?"

"Please, Becca," Dante said.

Marcus said, "Curl your fingers, if you can." I did this as he spoke. "Reach up and forward–"

Dante convulsed and groaned, then froze, a man trying really hard not to come.

"That's his prostate gland, I bet," Marcus said. "Try and hit that."

"Damn it," Dante gasped.

"Marcus," I said. "Tell me what he looks like, with my

169

fingers in his ass."

Marcus grabbed my left hand, the one with no glove, and put it on his cock. Even through latex, he felt scalding hot and harder than the dildo. "Rub it while I tell you," he said. "Dante! You want to know what you look like?"

"Hurry the hell up," Dante said.

"I bet you like waiting," Marcus said. "He's sweating, Becca – can you smell it?"

The whole room smelled like sweat, but Dante's – and Marcus' – was closer. "Yes."

"He's got his hands full of pillows and he's squeezing them like you're squeezing my cock. His shoulders are all clenched up and he's pressing his forehead into a pillow like that's going to make him come."

I knew that feeling. I twisted my fingers a little inside Dante's ass and felt him clench hard.

Marcus said, "And he's humping a pillow, just a little. Naughty," he said, and I heard a smack, and felt the vibration of his hand hitting Dante's ass cheek.

"Hurry up!" Dante said.

I gave Marcus' cock one last long stroke, feeling him arch to follow it, like a cat. Then I held out my hand for the dildo.

Marcus gloved my hand first, then lubed it, and finally laid the dildo across my palm. It was shorter than a real cock, and less thick, but it had a realistic shape, circumcised and with a ridge down the back. At the back end, it flared out into a base. Marcus said, "That's to fit it into a harness," and I shuddered, thinking of what that might feel like.

Dante was waiting. I considered how to get the thing into him and finally decided to hold his rim open with my fingers and work the dildo in from there, working my fingers out gradually. This worked. At least, Dante huffed and groaned and said, "More!" whenever I asked.

At last, the base was pressed flat against his ass, and the dildo was all the way in. I pulled down on it, hoping to bump his prostate again, and was rewarded by a deeper groan than I'd heard yet. "Oh, yeah," Marcus whispered in my ear. "Keep it up. Don't pull it out, just ride it."

Marcus got behind me, straddling Dante's legs, and rocked his cock against my back while I worked the dildo in Dante. Dante sounded like he was dying with every push, and I could feel him straining up off the pillows, trying to drive the dildo in further, like me when I was getting fucked. I wanted to fuck him fast and hard, yank it out and jam it in – was that how men felt? – but I couldn't because it would hurt him. I settled for pushing the base of the dildo a little harder, and a little harder, until Dante was coming, for sure he was coming, he screamed. I'd never heard a man scream like that.

"Fuck," Marcus said. "Can I fuck you now? Right now?"

"Please," I gasped, falling forward onto Dante's heaving back as Marcus manhandled my hips and plunged into my pussy. I was coming before he was all the way in, and it only took him three hard, short strokes.

We lay there, all three of us in a pile, gasping, then Marcus pulled out and rolled off me, and I scrambled off Dante, who weakly threw his arm over me.

Dante said, sleepily, "We're doing that again. Right?"

"Right," Marcus said.

"Next time Marcus is going to fuck you," I said.

The Librarian
by Eva Hore

'Hi Sheila, it's just me,' I said, bursting through the front door. I was running late for a dinner date with my sister, Christine.

I stopped dead in my tracks as I spied her coming out of the bathroom. I'd never seen her looking so hot. She nervously brushed a few wisps of hair that had escaped from beneath a towel that was twisted into a turban on her head, clearly unnerved that I'd seen what she was wearing.

'I … er …I didn't expect you home so early,' she stuttered.

I couldn't keep my eyes off her stunning figure. She was wearing a red and black teddy underneath her robe. It was open, revealing her amazing body. She had beautiful ebony skin and the red complemented her, turning her into a vibrant vamp.

'I forgot something,' I said, still staring at her breasts.

She pulled the robe tight around her body and rushed into her bedroom. I stood there looking after her. In the twelve months we'd shared this apartment, not once had I seen her go out on a date, yet these last five Fridays, whenever I got home, she was never here and didn't arrive back until Sunday morning.

When I'd asked her where she'd been, she just said she'd been out with some old school friends. I suggested she bring them around here one Friday. I said I'd love to meet them, but she just ignored me.

I was a snoop by nature and the fact that she had that sexy teddy on didn't fool me. Normally she dressed very conservatively. She was a librarian and believe me, usually she looked the part. Hair pulled up in a bun, horn-rimmed glasses. She looked and acted like a mouse.

On the weekends prior she would just bum around in tracksuits and sloppy clothes. She always had her nose in a book. I must admit I didn't have much time for her, always busy with my own life. I had no idea she was so horny-looking.

She was seeing someone, but who? And why the secrecy?

'See you,' she yelled, as she passed my door.

I felt so alone when she left. I lay on my bed thinking about her. Dinner with Christine now seemed such a chore whereas before I was looking forward to it.

'Can we skip dinner?' I asked Christine when she answered her phone.

'Yeah, why?' she said.

'Oh, I just don't feel like it that's all,' I said.

'You okay?' she asked.

'Yeah, it's just that…it's...'

Christine knew I had a crush on Sheila. She'd already told me to either tell her or get over it.

'It's what?' she pried.

'It's Sheila. She's going out again tonight and I caught her coming out of the bathroom wearing a very sexy teddy,' I blurted out.

'So what! Leave the girl alone. You have to get over this obsession you have with her,' she said.

'I'm not obsessing. I'm just curious. Don't you think it's strange, her spending all those weekends away and not telling me anything.'

'I think you're strange. She doesn't have to tell you

174

anything. You're not her mother. Don't bug her about it. It's her own business. I've got another call. I'll talk to you tomorrow,' she said hanging up.

I rolled over burying my face in the pillow. I didn't care what she said. I wanted to know what she was up to. Many thoughts and scenarios rushed through my mind. I lay there thinking hard, wondering where she was and what she was up to.

I imagined that I'd followed her out, watched as she ran down the steps, her long hair trailing after her. She'd hop into a cab and her coat would ride up so I'd be able to see the tops of her stockings. Stockings meant suspenders and suspenders meant no ugly pantyhose.

I'd keep my distance as the taxi sped through the quiet streets. It would stop in a seedy part of town where there were old warehouses. I'd cut my lights and idled along, just like in the movies. When she knocks on a door someone wearing a dark robe will answer it.

I can't see what the person looks like as the light from inside the room shadows his face. She slips inside and I'm left to wonder what to do next. I decide to cruise by slowly; my lights still off and park just around the corner of the building.

What would happen next?

Faint music would be coming from inside. There are windows but they are too high for me to see into. Skirting around the back I'd find an old milk crate. I take it with me back to a window and balance carefully on it. I'm able to peer inside, just between the crack of the curtain.

This room is a dining room. A huge wooden table dominates the room with large, ornate chairs that could seat about twenty people. Nothing at all mysterious about this room, quite boring actually and then I see someone walk past the room so I'd pull back on instinct, become more interested and grab my crate and go to the other side.

Can't have my fantasy too boring. I'd have to make it

175

more exciting.

This room would be nothing like the other. This one is decked out with what looks like thick and luxurious carpet, with deep mahogany furniture and plush red velvet covers. There is a huge chair, more like a throne, placed at the centre of one of the walls. Small tables and armchairs are scattered about the room.

Large wooden posts are attached to the ceiling at the same end as the throne and there is a crate or cage with wooden bars nearby, an array of whips adorn the wall and in a glass cabinet I spy dildos, vibrators and other interesting toys.

Yes, that gives it a definite intriguing atmosphere.

Voices alert me to the doorway. Sheila is leading the way, wearing a long purple robe. As she walks, the gown parts and underneath I see she is still wearing the sexy teddy and definitely stockings and suspenders. Her hair is draped around her like a shawl. Even from this distance I'll be able to see she has her face beautifully made up and as she heads for the throne, others will enter the room. All will be women.

Sheila will be the only one in purple. She'll stand out, look special. Some will have black, some red and two girls will sit at Sheila's feet wearing white tunics, white see through tunics. I'll peer harder, nearly topple off the crate to see if either of them are wearing underwear.

They won't! Dark nipples will stand out like beacons as the girls cross their legs to sit on the floor. Most of the armchairs will be taken up. Waitresses, dressed only in a short apron and nothing else, their breasts swaying as they walk will enter as well as two men wearing tight leather pants and no shirts. They'll stand on either side of the girls who are at Sheila's feet, their arms crossed, muscles flexed.

My pussy throbs as I plan which way to go from here.

I'd be intrigued for many reasons. Firstly, that Sheila would be the head of anything as she is normally such a mouse. Secondly, that women would dominate this room. They'd have to be part of some sort of association, which definitely has nothing to do with the library association. Thirdly, naked female waitresses will serve drinks to women who slap them on the arse or pinch their breasts. They'll be so submissive that they show no reaction.

My hand steals down to my pussy and I feel the heat emancipating from there and I smile. This is the randiest I've felt for ages.

I can't hear what is being said, the walls would obviously be sound-proofed to keep away nosy people like me and I can't even imagine what they would say anyway. The two men will walk from the room and minutes later come back, both holding the arm of a beautiful young woman who they stand in front of Sheila.

I need to add some drama to this.

Some sort of heated argument will ensue and their body language will be tense. The woman will struggle to move away but the men will hold her firmly in their grasp. Sheila will approach the woman, look her up and down as though she is for sale. One of the girls who had been at her feet will hand her a cushion. Something will be resting on it.

It will be a knife.

Sheila will run the blunt edge of the knife down the side of the girl's face, over her neck and the swell of her breasts. Then down and under her shirt where with one quick upward motion she'll slice off the buttons and the shirt will fall open. The two men will rip it from her arms and discard it onto the floor.

I really should get into this sort of stuff; it's definitely a turn on.

Now they'll hold her arms more firmly as she begins to struggle. I'll watch mesmerized, as the knife moves under her bra straps and slices through them. Her bra will fall forward exposing a luscious pair of breasts. Now Sheila will trace the knife around her nipples before lowering her head to suck one into her mouth.

She'll laugh while the girl struggles against the men. One of the girls in the white tunic will remove the woman's skirt until she is standing in only her panties and cut up bra. Her gorgeous breasts will be heaving as she continues to struggle.

Sheila will place the tip of the blade at the edge of her panties and slowly inch its way down to the crutch. She'll rip her panties off and with a quick slice into the centre of the bra the woman will stand before her naked.

The woman's body is beautiful. She has dark black hair that hangs over her face as she continues to struggle with the men. Her pubic hair is also dark and stands out against her pale white skin. She'll have a perky arse and long muscular legs.

If this fantasy was real I'd want to go in there and throw myself into the woman's pussy. With all those other women in the room watching me I'd let them rip off my clothes and have their way with me. That scenario will be for another fantasy though.

I'd be so hot watching that I'd carefully slip out of my panties and quickly stuff them into my bag. I'd run my hand over my mound and pussy before sliding a finger into my wet slit. That would feel so good. I'd throw my bag over my back to allow me the use of both hands as I pull back the hood of my clit, smearing some of my juices over it and begin to gently rub it.

My attention will be drawn back to the activities at hand and while fingering myself I'd watch as they lashed her to something on the floor. A waitress is on her knees in front of a woman whose black robe is open, revealing her nakedness underneath. The woman slings one leg over the arm of the chair and the waitress will use a vibrator to stimulate her. Then she'll lower her head; her tongue will flicker out to lick her. The woman will grab the back of her head and draw her in closer, before collapsing back on the chair to enjoy.

While this is going on the two guys will hoist their capture up to what looks like a rack after they have already spread-eagled and tied her to it. They hook the pulley ropes to one of the pillars and then move away.

Sheila will walk around her to admire her body, her fingers trailing over her skin. She'll have a small whip in her hand, and she'll stand in front of the girl, smacking it into the palm of her other hand as though to frighten her. Something is being said but I'll have no idea what. Then she'll lash at the girl's breasts while she begs for her to stop.

This is turning me on. I smear my juices over my clit and rub hard, enjoying the rawness of it all. I'd never been whipped or spanked, well not like that, and I'm finding it quite a turn on, imagining what it would feel like.

Sheila will continue to whip the girl and I will see faint welts rising over her body before she falls to the floor in front of the girl and begins to lick her and I'll be so turned on just by thinking how my mousy flat mate would be into this sort of thing as I balance precariously on the crate.

Her tongue will roam over the girl's body before she stands and retrieves the whip. She'll take the handle and probe it into her pussy and I'll watch, licking my lips, as she inches it in and then begins to fuck her with it. This will all be too much for me and my juices will run down the inside of my thigh.

Now all the women in the black robes rise and come towards the girl on the rack. Their hands will be all over her, pawing at her breasts, fingers in her pussy and her hole, mouths licking every part of her. The men will not move from their position and from what I can see they certainly won't have hard-ons. I'll assume them to be gay! How could you not be turned on by that display?

I can't see much; their bodies will block my view. I'd be so turned on that I'd lean my back against the wall and rub my clit harder, bring on a powerful orgasm and secretively hope that someone is watching me. I'd be as horny as hell. I'd want to see my girlfriend Louise but would be hesitant to leave.

An approaching car will make the decision for me. I'd jump from the crate and hide around the back. The car will drive past though, not even slow down. I'd be pretty sure that this is where Sheila has been going every Friday night and know I can always come back every Friday night to watch. I'd need some relief so I run back to my car to visit Louise.

The desire to be fucked and the thought of Louise wearing her big black dildo has me driving like a maniac. I don't tell her what I've witnessed but Louise is wondering why I'm so randy when I practically tear her clothes from her and demanded a good fucking.

The thought of fucking Louise right now nearly has me putting a stop to this fantasy but I want to continue on, to play it out to the end.

We'd spend the night and the next day locked in each other's arms but I make sure I'll be home early Saturday night so I'll be fresh for Sunday morning. I'll confront Sheila about her sexuality and I'll definitely want to see her naked so I'll have to come up with a plan.

I'd be nervous. Butterflies would flutter around my stomach as I bathe and make myself up. I wouldn't be quite sure how to go about it, and by the time Sheila does come home, the thought of ravishing her body will be the only thing in my mind.

'Have a nice weekend?' I'd ask, as she tries to sneak in.

'Oh, you're up,' she'd say, stating the obvious.

'Yeah. Thought I'd get up early and welcome you home,' I'd say.

'Why?' she'd ask.

I'd rise from the couch and walk towards her. Her eyes would be open wide; her tongue licking at her beautiful, full

180

lips. I'd lift my hand and release the clasp from her hair. It would fall around her shoulders and I'd remove her glasses and place them on the table. Slowly I'd unbutton her coat, slip it down her arms to reveal her sexy teddy that she'd still be wearing.

She'd stand there breathing hard as I soak in her beauty. I'd run my hand down the side of her face and grab the nape of her neck. I'd pull her back by the hair and kiss the hollow of her throat. She'd reward me with a low moan of pleasure.

My tongue will seek out a nipple as I pull her hair back harder. I'd flicker my tongue around, draw it into my mouth to suck on as my fingers roam her abdomen; her mound, and then I'd cup her pussy.

She'd grab at me, pull me into her body as her tongue kisses my mouth with such passion. My hands will be all over her, pulling at her stockings, tearing them in the process, while I try to undo her teddy. She'll laugh, push me away from her, and wiggle her way out of it.

She'll stand there before me only in her ripped stockings and stilettos. I'll lay her down on the white couch, her dark skin standing out beautifully against it. I'd run my hands over her body, cup her beautiful breasts, lick at her dark nipples, smother myself into her cleavage before my hands go down further, into her kinky pubic hair and down to her slit.

I'd open her up like a flower, her outer lips will be like soft petals, her scent intoxicating as my nose nuzzles against her clit. Her hands will massage my scalp, pull me closer to her as the tip of my tongue runs over a stud that will be pierced through her clit.

Her long legs will wrap themselves around my head, crushing me while I devour her. I'll pull back to feast my eyes on her while I quickly slip out of my own clothes. I'd lie on top of her in the 69 position, my legs straddling her head.

*I quickly remove my clothing so I can touch myself,
massage my breasts, finger myself while I think about what
I'd do to her if she was really here in my bed with me.*

I'd be fascinated by the colour of her dark skin and hair
against my own light complexion and blonde hair. My hair
would fall over her mound and for a moment the contrast of
our colours would hypnotize me. She would pull at my
hips, try to drag me down. Her scent will waft up to me,
awaken me and I will ground my face into her, allow her
juices to smear over my cheeks, lips, chin and mouth.

We'd ravish each other, pleasing, as only women know
how. Later we'd lie on the couch locked in each other's
arms.

'How did you know?' she'd asked.

'I didn't,' I'd lie.

'I didn't want you to know,' she'd say.

'Why?' I'd ask.

'Every time I live with a girl, their girlfriends always get
jealous and I'm asked to leave. So I decided this time to
play it cool, hide who I really was,' she'd say.

'I can understand why people would get jealous of you.
You're beautiful,' I'd whisper into her hair, as I'd hold her
tight.

'Come with me,' she'd giggle. 'I've got something to
show you.'

She'd lead me into her room and I'd watch her sexy arse
sashaying provocatively before me. She'd lay me on her
bed and retrieve a box from underneath.

'See anything in there that you like?' she'd ask.

It would be full of dildos and sex toys. Some I've never
seen before. I'd pull out a huge black one with a tickler
attached. I'd lift my eyebrows indicating I'm interested.
She'd laugh and strap it on.

I'd lie back on her bed; my legs open and she'd kneel
before me. She'd probe my outer lips, I'd reach up to pull
her to me, kiss her hungrily on the mouth. I'd be able to

taste myself on her lips and I'd grab her by the arse so the dildo could ram into me. She'd be amazing, having mastered the strokes so that in no time I'd be coming.

Oh, the thought of her and the dildo had me rubbing my clit wildly, my back arching as an orgasm builds up.

Then she'd roll me over, hoist up my hips and have me in the doggy position. This way the dildo would reach into the very depths of me, hitting my g-spot while the tickler tantalized my hole.

She'd be an amazing lover and we'd spend the whole day in bed together. Later, while lying in the bath I'd want to broach the subject of her weekends away.

'So does this mean your Friday nights will change?' I'd ask.

'I don't see why,' she'd say, allowing soapy bubbles to slide over my breasts as her hands caress me.

'I just thought maybe we could spend more time together?' I'd ask.

'We have all week,' she'd say evasively.

'Yeah, I know,' I'd say. 'But what if I want to take you out somewhere?'

'We'll talk about it when the time arises,' she'd say. 'What about Louise?'

'What about her?'

'You'll still see her, won't you?'

'Of course,' the thought of a threesome would be uppermost in my mind.

'Good,' she'd say, 'I don't want to spoil what we've got either. Our living together has always been comfortable.'

I'd wonder why she wouldn't mention the warehouse and the group she is involved with. I wouldn't care. I'd hope that one day she'd initiate me into their ways. The thought of being tied up and at her mercy would definitely appeal to me. It would appeal to Louise, too.

Louise. Still sexually aroused I pull myself away from this fantastic fantasy and decided to ring Louise.

'Hello,' she said sleepily.

'Oh, sorry. Did I wake you?' I asked.

'What's wrong?' she wanted to know.

'Just wondering if you'd like some company. Thought we might pull out your box of toys and have some fun tonight.'

'Do you know what time it is?'

'No, what?'

'It's four in the morning,' she said.

'You're kidding,' I said, truly surprised.

I didn't realise my fantasy had gone on for so long.

'I'm feeling horny,' I said.

'Obviously,' she laughed. 'Hurry up and get yourself over here then.'

We had the best sex ever that night and from now on I intend to conjure up lots of fantasies, thought I might even write about them, see if I can get them published. Let other people enjoy them as much as I did inventing them.

Maggie
by Kay JayBee

Maggie peered through the crack in the barn door, wondering if the whispered rumours were true. She was worried for them; the villagers could be a formidable force if they turned on you, and the reaction from the church would be truly terrifying. Maggie knew she was risking her own damnation by even thinking about it, but she couldn't help it, the idea of them fascinated her.

Creeping behind the back of the charcoal burners hut, the men disappeared into the woods. Previously Maggie had only known them as belonging to the huge category of people that made up 'her betters,' but now she'd heard them call each other Peter and John. Hesitating for a second, Maggie looked carefully around, wary in case others were watching, and then, slipping away from her work, she followed.

Maggie had learnt to move through woodland without making a sound from an early age, an essential skill when bagging rabbits with her widowed father. She'd grown up a lot since those younger days, forced to act as a replacement for her mother as keeper of the house, whilst working on the farm, preparing meals, and ignoring the constant put-downs from her father. Maggie lived increasingly in fear of him and under the shadow of an unsympathetic church, which was constantly suspicious of any girl with a quick tongue and an enquiring mind.

Maggie knew she was wicked. Nearly every night as she lay behind the makeshift curtain which separated her from her brothers, as they slept on the straw covered attic floor, she let her treacherous fingers stray between her parted legs, up towards her ripe brown nipples and back again, driving herself to a state of exquisite but silent delight with the lightest of touches, acquiring herself a one way ticket to hell. As she lay beneath her rough blanket night after night her mind filled with forbidden images as she longed for a husband to be found for her to supply her needs, to save her from herself, and to take her away from the constant demands of her family.

She paused by the thick trunk of an oak tree and listened hard. They were out of sight now, but faint sounds ahead guided her forwards. The trees were thicker here, the woodland unmanaged. Maggie stiffened and her heart pounded in her chest as she heard a stifled groan. What were they doing? She crept forward, keeping her body low to the ground.

Finally she caught sight of her quarry, almost hidden behind some as yet un-coppiced beech trees, just beyond a small clearing. Maggie stuffed her sleeve into her mouth to prevent herself crying out. Somehow she'd known it would be true.

Years of conditioning had told Maggie she should be disgusted, outraged. She had imagined herself ready to pile in with advice, to beg them to stop and save their souls. Instead she felt her nipples harden and an unmistakable tingle spread between her legs. They were kissing as tenderly as any young lovers. She couldn't tear her eyes away. Naked from the waist, hose pushed down to their shoes, each fondled the others stiff cock with one hand, whilst they, oblivious to her voyeuristic presence, murmured into each other's mouths with insistent, probing tongues.

Maggie slipped a hand inside her rough brown dress, and hastily rolled down the bindings that held her chest, partially freeing her breasts. 'So,' she thought with envy, caressing her hard nipples, her body responding to the sight before her, 'that's what it's like to be in love'.

The younger man, John, was kneeling down now, his mouth slipping over and around the tip of his partner's dick. Licking, teasing and coaxing, as Peter wriggled his fingers through John's hair to steady himself, his hips thrust as far forward as they would go. Maggie hardly dared even breathe in case she was spotted, but as Peter groaned his urgency increasing, she lost concentration and stepped back. A twig snapped beneath her flimsy leather shoes. John pulled back. He sat up, alert, pulling his partner down to the ground, covering his mouth to stifle his moan of loss. 'There's someone there' he whispered. Both men looked panicked; terrified. They knew the price for what they did.

Maggie saw their faces and immediately understood their horror as they grabbed at their discarded garments. Madly she rushed forward, babbling, unthinking, 'No, it's alright. I didn't mean to scare you. I'm sorry I found you, but, oh, you looked so beautiful together. I know it's wrong to watch, but don't be afraid I won't tell anyone, I promise I won't.'

The men looked at her in horror. 'Who are you? What are you doing here?' John turned to Peter, he spoke bluntly, all trace of his previous gentility gone. 'We will have to kill her.' Peter nodded. It was so obvious, why hadn't she thought of that? Stupid girl. Perhaps her father was right after all, maybe she was useless.

'No, please, Sirs. I'm Maggie, Sirs, I'm the farm labourer's daughter', she begged, rashly continuing, 'it was so lovely. Please, I won't tell anyone.' Neither man moved; could they trust her? They seemed to notice her dishevelled clothes for the first time. 'What were you doing while you were watching girl?'

'Oh please, Sirs,' cried Maggie, her face turned beseechingly from one to the other, before she became wary of her status, and humbly lowered her gaze and mumbled, 'I know I'm bad, but I can't help it, it feels so nice, and watching you I...'

Peter cut in, 'They say we are the wicked ones, Maggie. What do you think?' John grabbed her chin and held it firmly, boring his own dark eyes into hers to evaluate her answer.

'I just think you are in love, Sir.' John let her go and carefully looked her up and down. Maggie felt as though he was analysing her very soul. He turned to his partner. 'I think she may be just what we've been searching for.' Peter was nodding slowly, as if considering something.

'Is she wet? Have we really turned her on?'

'I'll see. Stand still, girl.' John commanded her in a voice used to giving orders. Maggie began to shake, fear and uncertainty flooded through her. Were they going to kill her? How would they do it if they did? What use could she be to them? The man called John was going to touch her. It was wrong, she would go to hell. Yet, despite her terror, her whole body was urging his fingers on.

Gripping a shoulder each, the men, grim faced, set to work on her body. John slipped his hand beneath the layers of her skirts, and recoiled slightly at her lack of undergarments. He nodded to his partner, 'She is indeed wet. Sodden. The girl is obviously a harlot.'

Peter frowned, but said nothing as he moved a hand down the top of her dress, causing Maggie to sigh beneath his hurried touch, her eyes wide at the effect of the illicit contact. In unspoken agreement, the men pulled the dress over her head and threw aside the bindings that remained crumpled beneath her tits.

Naked before them Maggie felt herself rooted to the spot under the heat of their inspective gaze. Certain that she was already well on her way to damnation, Maggie knew she didn't want to run, and her impatience grew as she mentally willed them to fall on her.

'If we do this,' Peter spoke to John, as if Maggie simply wasn't there, 'one of us can marry her. It would all stop, the gossip, the looks. One of us at least would be accepted, which would certainly help the other one. Yes? We do agree that the inconvenience of having to service a girl occasionally would be worth it?'

John nodded, they had considered acquiring a token wife before, but they needed a woman they could trust, someone who wouldn't go running off to the local priest at the first moment's freedom. Having a prisoner for a wife would simply be too tiresome and lead to more local interest, not less. He looked critically at the shivering girl. 'She is very low born; the farm labourer's daughter. Questions would be asked. Marriage by rape is one thing, but it is generally conducted between the correct classes.'

Maggie's chest was aching through lack of attention as she stood, her eyes still cast down, waiting for their next move. The hush seemed to go on forever as Peter considered John's words, before he finally spoke, 'We could pretend it was a genuine love match. I'm sure she could convince people of that, especially if her life depended on it.' He turned to Maggie, 'Could you, girl?'

'Oh yes, Sir' she stammered, wishing she had the courage to say 'Touch me, it wouldn't be rape, I want this.' She was yearning so hard for them to stroke her, smooth her, do something, anything, that she was afraid she might howl out in frustration and alert the whole village.

'It has to be you,' John spoke to his lover over Maggie's head. 'You have more experience with women.'

Peter nodded gravely, gripped Maggie by the shoulders and, without preamble, began kissing her savagely. If John hadn't moved behind her and clasped his smooth un-calloused hands around each breast, Maggie would have sunk down under the ferocious mouth. After initial shock of

189

the longed for onslaught, she kissed Peter back as hard as she could, her mind bursting with all the illicit fantasies she'd ever had as their teeth clashed together.

Peter broke away, his breath was short as he instructed John, 'Rub your fingertips over her nipples, she'll love that, we want her to be willing after all.'

Clumsily at first, John did as he was bidden, and slowly began to caress each teat, watching with fascination as they puckered beneath his touch, sending waves of desire coursing through Maggie's body, and forcing mewing noises from her lips. John continued to inflame her chest as Peter bent down and ran a finger between her slick legs. Maggie whined with pent up lust as she rubbed herself against his extended digit.

'She's nearly there, keep going.' John quickened the pace of his kneading whilst Peter flicked at her nub with one long rough finger, whilst slowly inserting another into her pussy, sending Maggie soaring into her first genuine orgasm.

The force of her release sent Maggie to her knees. She threw her hands over her mouth to stifle the scream climbing up her throat. The two men grabbed at each other above her crouched, come racked body, their initial caution at being observed forgotten in their renewed need for each other, both turned on far more than they had expected by the creature that had fallen beneath them.

Momentarily abandoned, Maggie sat between their legs, panting for breath, her bare legs scratched by the bracken-covered ground, as she inspected the bulges in the men's hose. Cautiously, she reached up, fascinated, and tentatively stroked the material that stretched over each set of balls. Their reaction was instant. Pulling apart, startled, they looked down at the incredible girl who smiled up at them, and continued to caress their taut bodies.

Peter stepped back slightly, checked in an unspoken enquiry with John, and pulled down his hose. Maggie didn't need to be told what to do, and instantly gobbled at the proffered cock. John watched as Peter closed his eyes, a look of indulgent pleasure on his face, before pulling off his own hose and, positioning himself behind Maggie, pushed his dick between her legs, robbing her eager body of the last traces of virginity. With blissful relief, she gasped for air around the thick shaft that crammed her mouth as she found herself filled to the hilt.

As he felt his own self-control ebbing away, Peter pulled out of Maggie's mouth, pushed her, back first, onto the splintered ground, with John still wedged between her legs. Peter pulled John's buttocks apart and jammed himself firmly between his flushed arse cheeks. He alone could see how deliciously sinful the three of them looked, and vowed that this would be a position they would take turns to adopt as often as possible.

Finally they had found a girl they could get used to, a girl whom could provide them the respectability they needed, and it appeared, would do anything they wanted, and he thanked God she'd discovered them.

Peter decided he would visit Maggie's father the following day. As Lord of the Manor his request to marry the girl would not be refused, and he'd go ahead anyway, even if it was. The gentle moans of satisfaction that drifted up from the ground beneath him, assured him that Maggie was more than satisfied with their plan. And she was.

Imagine great sex on your doormat every month!

- Imagine a new Xcite book landing on your door mat every month.
- Imagine reading the twenty varied and exciting stories that each book contains.
- Imagine that three books are absolutely FREE as is the postage and packing.

**No hassles
No shopping
Just pure fun**

Yes! that's the Xcite subscription deal –
for just £69.99 (a saving of over £25) you will get 12 books
with free P&P delivered by Royal Mail (UK addresses only)

All books are discreetly and perfectly packaged
Credit cards are billed to Accent Press ltd

Order now at www.xcitebooks.com
or call 01443 710930

Also available from Xcite Books:
(www.xcitebooks.com)

Sex & Seduction1905170785price £7.99
Sex & Satisfaction1905170777price £7.99
Sex & Submission1905170793price £7.99

5 Minute Fantasies 11905170610price £7.99
5 Minute Fantasies 2190517070Xprice £7.99
5 Minute Fantasies 31905170718price £7.99

Whip Me1905170920price £7.99
Spank Me1905170939price £7.99
Tie Me Up1905170947price £7.99

Ultimate Sins1905170599price £7.99
Ultimate Sex1905170955price £7.99
Ultimate Submission1905170963price £7.99